THE BIG TREE OF BUNLAHY

HERE WAS THE OLD CLOCK-MENDER, SEATED UNDER THE BIG TREE,
WITH PATCH THE NAILER AND MARTIN THE WEAVER BESIDE HIM.
I CAME OVER, AND I WAS THERE WHEN THE CLOCK-MENDER TOLD
THE STORY.

THE BIG TREE
OF BUNLAHY

Stories of My Own Countryside

PADRAIC COLUM

Illustrated by JACK YEATS

* * *

CLUNY
Providence, Rhode Island

CLUNY MEDIA EDITION, 2022

This Cluny edition is a republication of the 1933 edition of
The Big Tree of Bunlahy, published by The Macmillan Company.

For information regarding this title
or any other Cluny Media publication,
please write to info@clunymedia.com, or to
Cluny Media, P.O. Box 1664, Providence, RI 02901

∗   VISIT US ONLINE AT WWW.CLUNYMEDIA.COM   ∗

ISBN: 978-1685951566

Cover design by Clarke & Clarke
Cover image: George Inness, *The Elm Tree*,
circa 1880, oil on canvas
Courtesy of Wikimedia Commons

CONTENTS

ILLUSTRATIONS

Here was the old Clock-mender, seated under the Big Tree, with Patch the Nailer and Martin the Weaver beside him. I came over, and I was there when the Clock-mender told the story.
(FRONTISPIECE)

Simon the Huntsman (PAGE 3)

ABOUT THE BIG TREE
OF BUNLAHY

* * *

BUNLAHY calls itself a village, but it isn't a village at all. What is it, then? Just a single row of houses facing a wall that shuts in the wood and pasture belonging to an old, deserted mansion. If there were two rows of houses, one facing the other, it might have the right to call itself a village. But there never was, and there never will be, two rows of houses in Bunlahy. And yet it is because Bunlahy has but the one row of houses (and you might count them on the fingers of your hands) that it got part of the great fame that it has. For they used to say of anything that was one-sided, "It's all on one side like the town of Bunlahy." People who were never in it, nor knew what province or county it was in, would say and hear the name of Bunlahy.

But there was another thing that raised it into fame. Outside the wall and right before the middle house is a great elm tree. A seat of big, smooth stones is around it, the stones resting on an earthen mound. The tree was there in my father's time and my grandfather's time, and it was there when my great-grandfather was a whistling boy. And people were always mentioning it. "I come from within ten miles of the Big Tree of Bunlahy," a man would say when asked where he was from. Or a woman would say to her daughter, "The first time I met your father it was by the Big Tree of Bunlahy." Or a traveling man would say, "You never heard a blackbird sing unless you heard him when you were sitting under the Big Tree of Bunlahy." I myself met a black soldier in the Himalaya Mountains, which are beyond the Red Sea, who said to me, "Do you know the Big Tree of Bunlahy? I often heard my father speak about it." And this will show you that fame is not only for the big and stirring things of the world; things that aren't big and aren't stirring get a share of it too, just as the little pools in grassy borders of the road are lighted by the same sun as the great rivers going through the land.

And perhaps it was because I heard so much about it that I'm back again in the place and sitting under the Big Tree of Bunlahy after having spent the two middle quarters of my life guarding Kings' palaces and searching for gold in the valleys of Van Diemen's Land. I remember coming into Bunlahy when I was as young as that little tree growing on the moss of the wall. It was to get two candles that I came; I had two eggs to pay for the candles,

SIMON THE HUNTSMAN

a brown egg and a white one, for money wasn't used much in those days. Well, I got the candles and a piece of sugar-stick for what was over from the price of them, and I came out from the shop that was at the very end of the row. The rooks and the jackdaws that were in the trees inside the wall were making more din than the people; old Patch the Nailer made a ringing sound as he hammered out a long nail on his anvil, and at the other end of the row there was the clack of Martin the Weaver's loom. The jackdaws were hopping about the hollows that they had their nests in, and saying, "ka, ka," as if they were trying to talk like people, and the big rooks that never lighted on house or wall but flew up to the very tops of the trees were saying "kaw, kaw," as if they had a speech of their own and didn't care whether people liked it or not. "Kaw, kaw," they said as they flew above the jackdaws that were on the wall and the lower branches of the trees. And by the big, deserted house that had Baron's Hall for name, the peacocks cried.

Under the Big Tree a man who belonged to that house was seated—old Simon the Huntsman, his scarlet coat on and an old hound lying on the ground beside him. He beckoned me as I came by; he wanted me to read a letter to him that he had just got. I sat beside him and I read it to him; the letter was from his son Jack, and it was to say that he took his pen in hand to write these few lines, hoping they would find his father in as good health as they left him at present, thank God, and that he would come to see him, if not this harvest then the next. When I had read it to him, he folded the letter and put it inside his coat. "One harvest and another harvest," he said, "but I'll be as old as Usheen and as lonesome by the time I see any of them."

Before he went one way and I the other way, he told me:

THE STORY OF USHEEN

Usheen with his three hounds went over the hill to hunt. A stranger-woman followed him and she was one that he had no fancy to look at, for her lip hung down, her hair was a tangle, and the nose was crooked on her face. She sang as she went on. Her song was about the Land of Youth, where no one loses strength nor beauty, and where the blossoms are always upon the trees. Usheen went on without hearing or heeding her singing.

She was from the land she sang about. She was Niav, the daughter of the King of the Land of Youth. Hearing of Usheen who lived in the green land of Eirinn, the son of Finn, the Captain of the Fianna, she had made up her mind she would marry no other man but him. She had gone down to the sea-shore; she had mounted her steed—a steed that could go upon the waves as one of ours could go upon a grassy course—and she had come to the green land of Eirinn-O.

But the elements of our land made a change in her; her lip hung down, her hair went into a tangle, the nose became crooked on her face. Sad and sorry was the daughter of the King of the Land of Youth when she looked at herself in a well under a whitethorn tree. She would have gone back to where everyone was fair and she the fairest of them all. But then she saw Usheen, the son of Finn the great Captain. And when she looked on him she knew that she would rather stay in Eirinn and be near him in all her bad looks than be in the Land of Youth where he would never be seen by her. So Niav put her steed in a cave by the sea-shore and went where she could watch the encampment of the Fianna.

She followed Usheen when he went across the hill with his three hounds. All day he hunted; she went where he went; with his spear, his sling, his hounds, he brought down boar, and birds, and deer. He wondered how he could carry all the game back to the encampment. Then Niav came from her hiding-place and stood before him.

When he saw the stranger-woman with her looks so ill-favored, he was for drawing away from her. But she spoke to him, and her voice was sweet. "Usheen," she said, "do not leave behind you any of the game you have brought down. Come, now. I will help you to carry it, and you may give me something for my service."

Then she took some and he took some of the game and they carried their bundles on their shoulders. And as she went with him down the hill she sang a song that was a delight to Usheen. When they came to the paling of the encampment, he said to her, "What would you have me give you for the service you have done me?" And she answered him and said, "A kiss, Usheen."

So sweetly did she say it, so gently and resignedly did

she bend her head, that the hero's heart was touched. He raised her head; he kissed her mouth. Then Niav bent her head again as if to hide the features he had looked upon; but her fingers still held his hand.

Once more she raised her head, and every feature of her face was beautiful like the sky after the change of dawn. "Who are you," he said to her, "who were so unlike what you are?" "I am Niav, the daughter of the King of the Land of Youth," she said.

They sat together on the top of a hill that seemed to them the top of the world. Usheen's companions came there looking for him. They would have laughed and mocked to see him with a girl's hand in his hand and the bundles of game beside them. But when they saw the beauty of Niav and her queenliness they were silent. They lifted the game on their shoulders and carried it back to the encampment.

All welcomed Usheen and Niav. Feasts were made for them, and Niav was treated like the queen of the world. But Usheen's companions were silent when they were with him, and no longer was there mirthfulness in the encampment. "The heroes are not the same since Niav came amongst us," said Finn to Usheen. "They think of her, and it is not well when many men think of one woman. Go with her, my son, to the place she came from."

That day when Usheen went to her, Niav said to him, "Now you must come with me to my own land." So deeply did he love her that he left all the men who had been companions to him, and left his father, and the hills and valleys of his own land. She called to her steed; it came to her out of the cave where it had been left; they mounted and rode away on it. They rode across the waves, and they came to Tir-nan-Oge, to the Land of Youth, where no one grows old, where rough winds nor rains never come, and where leaves and blossoms are always on the trees. It was happy in that land. Usheen had everything his heart could wish for, and his youth and strength remained ever the same. One day he said to Niav, "I have a wish to go back to Eirinn and see my father and my companions, and the hills and valleys of that land again."

She wept when she heard him say this. "How long do you think it is, Usheen, since we left Eirinn together?"

"It is three years," he said.

"It is three hundred years," said Niav, "since you came to the Land of Youth with me."

He wept when he thought on all that must have happened in Eirinn in that great stretch of time. He would have to know what had happened and know what memory was left of Finn and the Fianna. He was happy no more in the Land of Youth. Then, seeing that his thought was gone to the hills and valleys of his own land, Niav gave him the steed that could travel upon the waves as upon a grassy course. When he was starting, she said to him, "You are going for a while only and so I can bear to let you go. But you can come back to the Land of Youth only if your foot never touches the ground of Eirinn. Do not dismount from the steed I give you. In the Land of Youth I wait for your return."

The steed carried him over the gray waves and to the green shore of Einnn-O, and Usheen rode upon the hills and through the valleys, seeking traces of Finn and the Fianna. No one that was like to any of them did he see in the land, and nowhere did he hear tale or tidings of them.

He knew that in a certain spot a trumpet was hidden. If any of the Fianna blew into it the rest of them would hear and come to the help of him who sounded it. Usheen rode to where this trumpet, the Borabu, was hidden. Before he went back to the Land of Youth he would sound it, he thought, and find out if any who had the tale of the old days would come to where he blew it. He rode to the great flag-stone under which the Borabu was hidden. A herdsman was in a field near by, and Usheen called to him. "Lift up the flag-stone," he said to him from his steed.

"Neither I nor twenty men like me could lift the flag-stone," the herdsman said.

Usheen rode to it; stooping down, he raised an end of

it. The Borabu was there. "Lift up the trumpet," he said to the herdsman, "and give it to me."

"Neither I nor three men like me could lift up the trumpet," the herdsman said.

Then Usheen flung the stone back, and, stooping from his steed, put his hand upon the trumpet. So eager was he to raise it that he let his hand touch the earth. The steed shook as if some strange appearance had come before it. The saddle-girth broke, and Usheen fell from the steed, down upon the ground.

Niav, in Tir-nan-Oge, knew what had happened to him when the steed came back to her. Usheen was more old and feeble now than anyone in the land; the herdsman who had seen a splendid youth mounted upon a bounding steed now saw an old, old man lying upon the ground. And all his companions were dead and gone, and their names were hardly remembered.

That was the story that he told me. Then old Simon with his scarlet coat on him went through the gate and up to the big, deserted house that the peacocks were crying beside, his old hound following him. And to be back in the house before the candles I was sent for were wanted, I had to run like a redshank.

OLD CUCKOO,
THE CLOCK-MAKER

* * *

SHORTLY afterwards I heard another story under the Big Tree. It was from the strangest of all the people who came, in my time, into the village. He was an old Clock-mender. He had bunches of brass clock-keys hanging round his neck, and he carried in his bag dozens and dozens of clock-faces; they were big and little, but they were all yellow, for they were the faces of clocks that would tick nor strike no more—clocks that were dead and done with. He was called Old Cuckoo. Maybe it was on account of the cuckoo in a clock, or maybe it was because he appeared at odd times and nobody ever knew where he came from, or maybe it was because he was so strange in every way—a half-crazy man. I think I was told that his wife had gone from him, and that was the reason he went from place to place; he was hoping to find her or get some word of her. Years before, I suppose, he had given up a little shop in some town to go round the country in this way. Well, here he was in Bunlahy, and seated under the Big Tree, with Patch the Nailer and Martin the Weaver beside him. I came over; I always came to listen when I saw Patch and Martin together. And I was there when the old Clock-mender told the story that I shall name:

THE FIRST HARP

UPON a time that was neither your time nor my time, a man and his wife were living at the back of the hills yonder. They had been happy together when they were young, but now that they were getting aged they were not so happy. Misfortunes had come on them, and each misfortune left them less and less forbearing with each other. So downcast did they become that they never went to a sport or a merrymaking; they got no new things to wear; they would look with surprise on people dressed in their best and going to amusements; they did not know when holidays came round: Hallowe'en would come, and they would have no apples to share with each other; Michaelmas would come, and they would kill no goose to feast themselves; May-day would come, and they would wonder to see the children going from door to door with flowers in their hands.

And if the goats strayed away and there was no milk for the supper, "It's because my husband doesn't mind what happens about the place that I've to eat dry bread tonight," the woman would say. And if she lost three halfpence out of the shilling she had got for something she sold in the market, the man would keep on blaming her for the rest of the day. On times like these they would sit in the house remembering the miseries that had come on her or on him through the other. When they had been pleased with each other they had made no account of these miseries, but now when they were not pleased they remembered nothing else. One night as they sat in a house that had no fire they began going over the times when they had comforts and when they could do pleasant things together. In everything one remembered there was blame for the other. They lay down, each thinking they would clear the score by forsaking the other. And in the morning each put a hand in the cold ashes of their hearth and went away from the house.

They came to the sea-shore, the man not knowing that the woman was behind him, and the woman not knowing that the man was before her. This is what befell the man that morning. He saw how the beach stretched away without a rock breaking through its yellow sand, and he saw how the clouds sailed above, big and white, without even a gull stretching its wings under them. The waves could not be seen, for the tide was very far out. There was no mark to go towards, but the man went on. Then he heard a sound and he went towards where it came from. It was a long, strong, soughing sound, and then it became a soft, sighing, sinking sound, and between the sinking and the swelling there were other sounds—a whirring sound and a whispering sound, a lifting sound and a lulling sound. He went on and on, and at last he came to what they came from. And lo and behold! there was a whale there, a great bulk upon the sands. But it was a whale that was only bones now; the flesh had been stripped off it, and the wind was going through its ribs and touching upon the slight bones that were like river-reeds inside the skeleton. And the sounds changing ever never ceased—soughing, whirring, whispering, sighing. He stood listening to the music and forgetting everything that was upon his mind. And he saw his wife standing at the other end of the whale's bulk with wonder in her looks as she listened to the sinking and the swelling, the lifting and the lulling music that the wind made through the bones of the whale.

They went back talking about the wonder they had come upon. They had a meal in their house and still they talked about the wonder. Together they did the work that had to be done while they listened to the sounds that they thought they could hear. One evening the man made a frame of pine-wood, strung strings loosely across it, and left it hanging in the doorway of the house. The wind

THEY LISTENED TO THE MUSIC THAT THE WIND MADE
THROUGH THE BONES OF THE WHALE.

made music on the strings. Then he had a dream; he
knew that pieces of wood across the frame would make
the sounds come stronger: he put two boards in the
frame, and the wind upon the strings had a deeper sound.

Neighbors came to listen; the man was praised for the
wonder he had made; rich people made gifts to the couple.
Then the man made a frame on which the strings were
drawn tightly; he made the sounds by striking his fingers
across the strings—louder and more piercing sounds. He

went from place to place playing this instrument, his wife going with him. The King of the land heard about the instrument and the player; the man was brought to play before him. Sickness and sleeplessness left the King—so much did the music do for him. And the man and his wife were given riches so that they might stay always with him. They lived there content with themselves and content with each other. And the instrument that the man made was called a Harp, and the man himself was Cend-find, the first Harp-player in Ireland.

In case you might think that I never knew a story except what was told to me, I'll tell you this one. You can say what you like about it, but you'll have to say that it was never told by anyone before, either under the Big Tree of Bunlahy or any place else.

NEVER TOLD BEFORE

* * *

OUR HEN

IT was a very quiet farm-yard. The Cock went to bed early and did only the amount of crowing he was expected to do. Some of the younger Hens had been in the habit of going out a little, but they had given that up, and never left the farm-yard now. The Guinea-hen went out; she went by herself to the little field that was beyond the yard, flew up on the rick of hay that was there, or roamed up and down by the hedges. The Turkeys were no gadders; they went out, of course, but they went to the same place day after day, and they never saw nor heard anything that was at all extraordinary. The Geese went more abroad than the Turkeys; they went right down the road, turned into the grazing field, and went often into the field beyond the grazing field. They said all they had to say just as they were turning into the yard, and then they had little more to say. To be sure, the Geese did a certain amount of cackling in the night and early in the morning, but the rest of the farm-yard had got used to that; besides, everyone liked having the Gander about; he was a good watchman, and he had even faced and frightened off a strange dog that had come prowling into the yard. The Ducks were ramblers; they went very far, and they went into very odd places, but they were regular in the way they went and came, and they were not at all disturbing. I nearly forgot to tell you that there was a Pigeon in the farm-yard. She had had a mate, and they used to fly away together, and when they were back they would stay on a roof and say "coo, coo" to each other. But she had lost her mate; he was killed while they were on an excursion. The Pigeon went on no more outings and gave up saying "coo, coo." She gave up flying, too; she just went around picking up things and staying a good deal in the barn. Everyone had been sorry for her, but now they didn't take notice of her at all. And, of course, there was in the farm-yard, as there is everywhere, someone who was looked down on. He was the Bantam. One of the younger Hens had lost her wits about him, and he had shown her that she was forcing her company on him. This Hen had become a little extraordinary; she spoke to no one now, and she roosted on the branch of a tree. No one spoke to the Bantam. Then there was a red setter-dog who slept in a kennel in the yard, but who did no work as a watch-dog.

OUR HEN

And there was Our Hen. She was called Our Hen, not because she was the only Hen, or because she was the oldest Hen there, but because she never did nor said anything that a Hen shouldn't do or say. Once she hatched out a brood of Ducklings; she was anxious about them, of course, and as long as they stayed in the farm-yard, getting into the puddles there, she stayed with them. Then they began slipping through a hedge and ducking themselves in the pool that was just outside the yard. Other Hens would have followed them out there. Not Our Hen. Something told her to stay this side of the hedge and warn them that what they were doing wasn't for their own good. They came back and took to the yard-puddles, and all the other

Hens who had reared broods of Ducklings said that Our Hen had shown the youngsters a good example by staying in the yard. They went into the pool again a while after went where the grown Ducks went. But by this time Our Hen had given up being troubled about them.

Now she had hatched out half a dozen chicks. They were little and they ran all over the yard. There was no denying they were wild little things—"very giddy," a Hen who had brought out a brood at the same time said of them. They were young Pheasants. But no one in the yard guessed that, for Pheasants had never been seen there. They ran all over the place, their heads raised, their eyes shining—they were greatly admired for their eyes. But although they were here and there through the yard while a duck was saying "quack," they were very good little things, and they would be back and under their Muime's wings the moment she called to them earnestly. I don't know who told them to call her that, and from the pool they "Muime," "Foster-mother," but that is what they always called her.

One summer day, when—

A Blackbird was singing,
"Oh, now you know my sort;
I'd rather have a guinea
Than a five-pound note.

And I'd rather have a daisy
Than your little stack of rye,
And I'd rather have a berry
Than I would a grove of spice.

And now you've heard my singing,
And now you know my sort,
Leave your golden guinea,
And take your five-pound note!"

That day the young Pheasants, grown now, went through the hedge and round by the pool that the Ducklings used to duck in. Our Hen did not leave them. "The children," she said, "are so very bright that they're sure to learn something." They were in a green field now. "Oh, Muime," said one of them, running up to her, "isn't the world a big place?" "Yes. One could easily get lost in it," said Our Hen; "tell the others to come back to me. They've gone every sort of way. Bring them back until I show them the Cow." The little Pheasant ran after the others. But by this time her brothers and sisters were everywhere through the field; with their bright eyes and their quickly turning heads they saw a hundred things. They went on and around, and here and there, picking at the grasses. Our Hen came on one of them, and then on another, but never on all of them together. Still, they were very good. She put one beside a big stone, and then another, and told them not to stir until she had got them all together. They did not stir. When Our Hen came back with the last chick, they were all crouching beside the stone. "Now, children," said she, "if you follow in good order and don't stray around, I'll show you everything in the world. Where would you like to go?" "Oh, Muime," said they, "couldn't we go where the Turkeys go?" "I wonder why you've such ideas," said Our Hen. "I don't believe I ever went that far myself. But you're such bright children that if you go to places you're sure to learn something. I'll take you along. But come back to where you were, for unless you stay all together we can't go anywhere." "Yes, Muime, we'll stay together," said the young Pheasants. "Is that the Guinea-hen that's up there? How did she get up there? Can the Guinea-hen fly?" "I never knew such creatures for noticing things," said Our Hen. "Now take things quietly, do. The Guinea-hen flies a little. As a matter of fact, we all can fly to some extent, but it isn't done. Don't be misled into trying to fly. It's so easy going astray when you start flying. But I'll tell you something about that when we get back. Don't be looking around so much."

They kept together and Our Hen kept with them, and they talked about this and that, and soon Our Hen was astonished to see how far they were from the farm-yard.

"I forget," she said, "whether the Turkeys go up or down when they come to this place." "Oh, Muime, they go this way," said one of the party; "we see their tracks. It's the Geese go the other way. What big tracks they make!" "I never knew anyone's children so bright as you are, I declare," said Our Hen.

So they went on, the young Pheasants running here and there, but coming together again, while Our Hen kept coming after them and explaining things to them. She herself was getting very excited about all the things that she found were in the world. Such long grasses! Such odd things with shells on them that moved! Butterflies, too! Little pools that were very nice to drink from! She would have to spend a lot of time explaining all they had seen to the chicks when they got back. It was all very different from the farm-yard. They came upon the Turkeys. Our Hen was surprised to see ones she knew so far away from home. And she was surprised that the Turkeys did not notice them; they went on picking at the bushes. "Oh, Muime," said the little Pheasants, "we think you're so good to have brought us so far! What a lot of things we've seen!" "Yes, but you're tired now, aren't you?" said Our Hen. "We'll stay here for a while and then we'll go back."

The little Pheasants crouched around her, and Our Hen had a snooze, for she was certainly very tired. She wakened up and they were all gone—not one was in sight. Our Hen got a terrible fright. She ought never, she knew now, take out chicks under a sky that hawks could come down from, and into places where creeping beasts could come up on them! She ran here and she ran there, calling them. She opened out her wings and ran along, clucking and clucking. And then she came upon them; one ran to her and another ran to her, and she counted them, and she found she had them all. "And now we'll go home," said Our Hen. But they were not listening to her; their heads were raised and were looking round in every direction, and they were saying "Muime, Muime," as if she were before them instead of behind them. So she ran up to them and went on with them, so out of breath that she couldn't cluck to them. They came to a place where there were houses. They went along by the wall facing the houses. There were trees there, and jackdaws were making a din in them. They went through a gap in the wall, and they were in the wildest place that ever anybody was in—trees that went up to tremendous heights; long grasses; Crows saying "kaw, kaw" very menacingly, rabbits hopping about. "Don't be frightened—don't be frightened," said Our Hen, "and I'll get you home." "Why, isn't this home, Muime?" they said as they went through the long grasses and into the ferns. "Oh, what lovely places! We didn't think there were such lovely places in the world! Oh, won't you live here with us always, Muime? We could fly up; we could find such nice places where no one would ever find us; we'd make such a nice nest in the ferns for you, Muime!" "Oh, I'm going to lose my head! I'm surely going to lose my head!" said Our Hen.

A huge creature rushed upon them. In an instant all the little Pheasants had hidden themselves. Our Hen, just before she gave in to her fright, saw that the huge, terrible creature was Pointer, the setter-dog that stayed in the farm-yard. Our Hen flew straight at him and made him get back. She was in a prime rage, I can tell you. "How dare you?" she said. "What do you mean by following us around and jumping at us like this? I'll get the Gander to chase you and beat you with his wings. You think because you're away from home that you can misbehave like this, but I'll tell everyone about your conduct. I'll never speak to you again. You're not better than a wild creature even though you live in our farmyard." Pointer drew back and then slunk away. The little Pheasants came out of their hiding-places and gathered around her. "Oh, Muime, we were so frightened," they said. "What would we have done if you hadn't been with us?"

Our Hen got them together, and they all started for home. They made no delay on the road, and it was wonderful how quickly Our Hen got along—running, fluttering, flying—the young Pheasants had to do their best to keep up with her. It seemed just one single rush between the wood and the lane to the farmyard. And just as they turned up the lane, they came on the Geese who were on their way home. Our Hen was so glad they were there. The Gander, as if he knew something had happened, lifted up his head and cackled, and marched behind them with his Geese. Our Hen felt safe at last. She and the little Pheasants kept just before the Geese until they were in the yard. The half-door of the barn was closed; Our Hen flew up on it and into the barn, and the little Pheasants flew in after her. No one was there but the Pigeon, and she was there so quietly that it was just the same as if no one at all was there.

"Now this, will be a lesson to you," said Our Hen to the little Pheasants. "You know now what the world is like. I don't ask you to be like the Pigeon who never sees anything, or goes anywhere, or talks to anyone, but I want you to make up your minds to be interested in what's at home. There's plenty to be seen in the yard, and you'll hear interesting things every day. After all, you're not Turkeys; you're not Geese; you're not Guinea-hens; you're not Ducks—you don't have to go outside." But even as she spoke to them, the little Pheasants were all over the barn, in corners and holes. They had already forgotten what had happened in the wood. And when Our Hen called to them they weren't there; they had found a hole in the wall and had gone through it, and were in the field behind the farm-yard. She got into a terrible state about it and ran up and down the yard just wailing. Then the Bantam whom nobody spoke to came up and told her where the chicks were. He was glad, of course, to have the chance of getting into conversation with Our Hen. It was he who went out into the field and commanded them to get back to the yard. They all came back. And then the Bantam stood on a stone and crowed. But nobody spoke to him or paid any attention to him.

When she came off the roost next morning Our Hen found the Pheasant chicks in a big coop that had wire across it. They were running up and down with heads twisting and bright eyes looking in every direction. "Oh, Muime, get us out of this—do, Muime," they cried to her. "Don't leave us here. We want to go with you into the wood again." But Our Hen could do nothing about getting them from behind the wire. She stayed beside them and talked to them in a low voice. The only thing they wanted to hear from her were stories about the travels they had been on and the wood they had gone into. When she told about these things, even the Pigeon and the Bantam and the Guinea-hen came up to listen.

Once Pointer came into the yard while Our Hen was telling about their adventures in the wood. She flew up on the coop and scolded him, and the Gander went right up to him and cackled at him, and Pointer had to sneak away.

In the coop the Pheasant chicks grew up, becoming taller and more beautiful every day. Two of them began to grow long tails and to have lovely feathers. They were the most beautiful children that ever were in the farm-yard—everybody had to agree when Our Hen said this. They were wild, she admitted; it was a strain they had got from her great-grandmother. But when they were out of the coop they would settle down like everybody else's children. The Bantam showed that he didn't believe this, but nobody paid any attention to the Bantam.

He had a lot to say to the young Pheasants when nobody else was around. He loosened the things that held the wire at one side of the coop, and then he told them to throw themselves all together at this place. They did. The wire pushed out, and the Pheasants, one by one, squeezed through and came out into the yard.

Our Hen was delighted, of course, to see them at their liberty again. She was a bit frightened, too. They were changed a good deal. She followed them about, admiring how they walked—so lordly! She was in an ecstasy about the lovely colors that were at the necks and on the breasts of two of them. Even the Turkeys talked to each other about them. And the Guinea-hen said that they were so good-looking that something told her they were not long for this world. Then she sank her head between her wings and fell into a state of great melancholy. But Mother Goose told her not to be nonsensical, for all would come right in the end.

Just as they were all talking like this, and Our Hen was scraping and scraping to get something really nice for them, something happened. The Pigeon said that she knew something was going to happen, and that that was the reason she went into the barn and stayed there all that day. Pointer came back. Everybody said he meant no harm, but as soon as he appeared one of the young Pheasants flew straight across the fence. It was a lovely flight—no one had ever seen anything like it. Then another flew and another, and they were all gone before the Guinea-hen lifted her head up.

Something told Our Hen that her children would never come back again. Without saying anything to anyone, she left the yard the next day for the second time in her life. She passed where the Turkeys were and hurried right on. She came to where the houses were. She went through the gap in the wall and into the wood. It was a terrible place, to be sure, but Our Hen made up her mind to be not in the least afraid of anything. She called to them and they came to her from under the ferns and from out of the bushes. "Will you come home?" she asked them. "Oh, but this is our home," they said, and Our Hen knew that they would go on believing that, and that she would never get them to go back with her. She stayed with them until it was getting dark, and all the time the Crows in the trees were saying dreadful things—about flying things being killed and deaths in the air.

She went back to the farm-yard and never left it again. Autumn came. The Crows went flying around. They wouldn't go home peacefully as they used to, but flew in different parties this way and that way. They would rise up out of the trees, and all the creatures in the farm-yard knew that something dreadful was going on in the wood where there were sounds like claps of thunder all day long. After this Our Hen took to roosting on a branch of a tree; she was under the Hen that had lost her wits. But Our Hen remained sensible. She didn't hatch any more, but she paid attention to the chicks that other Hens had hatched out, and she told them stories—stories about the distances she had gone beyond where the Turkeys went, and about her beautiful children that had a strain from her great-grandmother that made them strange and remarkable. She was never mournful like the Guinea-hen. And in days afterwards she was very kind to the Pigeon and even to the Bantam, always talking to them and very often speaking up for them when the others ran them down.

THE SHOEMAKER'S DAUGHTER

* * *

THE gentlemen who had been shooting came out of the
broken gate of Baron's Hall, three of them, carrying bags
in which were shot birds—pheasants. I had come into the
village that day with some message from my grandmother
to Kevin the Shoemaker. Well, I was spoken to by one of
the gentlemen and asked could I find him someone who
would repair his game-bag—its side was ripped open. He
gave me sixpence for the trouble I was being put to, and
I thought that a man who had gifted me with sixpence
when a penny was all that a boy could expect was very
rich and very noble; if there were more like him going
through our parts, I felt, we'd have people to look up to
and the lots of all of us would be bettered a great deal. He
was a young man beside the two other men and he was a
tall and a handsome man beside their commonness of size
and looks. "Sir Harry Wildair," I heard one call him, and
I thought that this was his real name, but I know now

GRACE

that it is a name out of a book. I took a hop, step, and a jump towards the Shoemaker's house, for I knew Kevin was just the man to stitch the bag properly; I'd have him come out and do the job where Sir Harry had laid the bag down on the seat under the Big Tree. But when I came out to the house who was standing behind the half-door and looking over it but Grace, the Shoemaker's daughter. I put all my breath into telling her about the tear in the gentleman's bag and about the need for getting Kevin out to put the stitches in it. "Don't speak so loud," said she, "anyone would think you were brought up in a mill." And then she said, "My father is doing a special bit of work now and he wouldn't like to be taken away from it. I'll go and stitch the bag myself." So she stepped back and took her father's long needle and her father's waxed thread and went to where the gentlemen were.

They were all very surprised by her appearance. I heard Sir Harry tell the others that he thought it well worth his while to have come to Ireland to meet a girl as lovely as this. I looked at her then, and for the first time I really saw the Shoemaker's daughter, Grace. She had a flowered kerchief pinned across her shoulders, and her hair was hanging over it. I saw that that brown hair of hers was lovely, and I saw that her brown eyes and straight nose and thin lips were very fine. She laughed as she held out the long needle and waxed thread to the three gentlemen, but it took her a long time to persuade Sir Harry Wildair to let her have his game-bag. He took the shot pheasants out of it and laid them on the seat and handed her the bag. She began to stitch it, standing beside the Tree, the three shooters before her and myself somewhere near. The younger man would have her talk about herself—who was in the house with her, what she did, and what countries she would like to go to. And she, to stop such talk, said that they would have to listen to a story. So as she put the long needle through the stiff stuff of the bag, making a seam with the waxed thread, she told a story that she named:

PADRAIC COLUM *

THE MAN WITH THE BAG

A man with a bag comes into this story. But before he
comes in let me tell you about the girl who was in the
house that he came to. She was named Liban, and well did
she deserve that name which means Beauty of Woman,
for her eyes were beaming, her mouth was smiling, her
cheeks were like roses, and her hair was brown as a cluster of nuts. And yet for all her beauty, Liban had little
chance of getting wed. Young men would come and ask
for her in marriage, but if they did her mother told them
they were first to climb a tree that overhung a high cliff
and take out of the raven's nest that was there a scissors
that the raven had carried off, and bring back in addi-
tion two of the raven's eggs. One young man and another
young man climbed the tree, but when he came to the top
branches that overhung the cliff and found them breaking under him, he got down from the tree and did not
go again to the door of the house. So Liban stayed beside
her mother's hearth and was likely to stay there, spinning
threads on her spindle while her mother spun them on
her wheel, and this was just what her mother wanted her
to be doing, for she got a deal of silver for all the thread
that she and Liban spun.

Well, it was to the door of this spinning-woman's
house that the man with the bag on his back came on a
morning. He asked for shelter. "And if you let me take my

34

rest here while I'm begging through the parish, I'll ask nothing else from you, ma'am," said he. "A good beggar doesn't ask for food where he gets shelter and he doesn't ask for shelter where he gets food. I know what a good beggar's conduct should be. My father was a beggar and his father was a beggar before him. I'm no upstart." The spinning-woman told him he could rest by the fire when he finished his round of begging in the evening, and when she told him this the man with the beggar's bag on his back turned from the door and faced the crooked lanes that went from house to house in the parish.

Liban looked after him as he went down the laneway, and she thought that only for the grime that was on him and the ragged clothes that he wore he would be good-looking enough. In the evening he came back, and his bag hung as if there was nothing in it. All the same, he refused the cup of milk and the cut of bread that Liban offered him. "All that I'll take in your house," said he, speaking to her mother, "is the place to rest myself and leave to put in your charge what I gained on my travels." And saying this he put his hand down in his bag and searched and searched there, and at last brought up what was there to be found. It was a pea. "I'll leave this in your charge and you'll be accountable for it," said he, "and if anything happens to it you and I will have to face each other in the Court of Dusty Feet. I'll take it back from you when I'm leaving your house." So Liban's mother took the pea and put it on the corner of her spinning-wheel, and the beggarman put the bag under his head and made ready to go to sleep. He sang a little song to himself. Liban liked it because a hazelnut came into it, and her other name (for she had another name) meant Kernel of the Nut. The song he sang as he put his head on the bag went:

> *The hazel in the dell—*
> *A nut with hoarding shell*
> *And sweet and white kernel.*

> *Can I have for my own,*
> *That nut so tight and brown,*
> *From the branch that I'll pull down?*

> *Can I take from its shell*
> *The sweet and white kernel*
> *Which will make all things well?*

Liban and her mother came out of the sleeping-room at the peep of day, and as they did the beggarman got up from where he was lying and opened the house-door and went off on his rounds, the crooked lanes of the parish before him. The girl went to get the breakfast ready. The little speckled hen that was her own came in to pick up the crumbs that would be around the table. She came as far as the spinning-wheel; she saw the pea; she stretched her neck up and picked it and swallowed it. "The pea that the beggarman left in your charge, my own little speckled hen has swallowed!" cried Liban. "He'll forget to ask about it," said the spinning-woman, "and as for you, take your spindle and get some threads done while the porridge is cooling."

But the first thing the beggarman said when he came to the door was, "Where is the pea that I left in your charge, woman of the house?" "A hen picked it up and ate it." "Which is the hen that ate the pea I left in your charge?" "The speckled hen that's before you." "That speckled hen is mine." "That cannot be." "It can be and it is, ma'am. It's the law, and if a beggarman didn't know the law, who'd know it?" And saying this he took up the hen that was picking from a dish and put her into his empty bag.

When he was going off next morning he took the speckled hen out of his bag. "I leave her in your charge," he said to Liban's mother. Then he went off, facing the crooked lanes of the parish, his empty bag hanging on his back. And so that nothing might happen to her, Liban made a little pen of wattles for the speckled hen, and tied her inside it. Then she took up her spindle. "I wish," said her mother, "that the beggarman had come to ask for you so that I might have him climb the tree." Liban was looking out of the door. She saw the pig beside the pen of wattles. The pen was strange to the pig, and she went rooting around it. The speckled hen flew into her mouth. The pig ate her. All that was left of the little speckled hen was the white feathers on the pig's snout.

And the first thing the beggarman said when he came in through the door was, "Where is the speckled hen that I left in your charge?" "The pig ate her," said the spinning-woman. "The pig is mine. That's the law, and if a beggarman doesn't know the law, who'd know it?" He went out into the yard then, took the pig by the leg, and dragged her into the house. He put her into his bag and tied its mouth up. Then he lay down in the corner with his head to the wool-sack, singing as he turned to sleep:

> *The hazel in the dell—*
> *A nut with hoarding shell*
> *And sweet and white kernel.*

> *Can I have for my own,*
> *That nut so tight and brown,*
> *From branch to be pulled down?*

> *Can I take from its shell*
> *The sweet and white kernel*
> *Which will make all things well?*

By the time the beggarman had left the house next morning Liban's mother had lost so much flesh through grief at the loss of her pig that she looked as if the weight of the pig had been taken out of her. And she wasn't able to eat her porridge, either. Liban took charge of the pig. She tied her to a bush under a wall of loose stones, thinking that no harm could come to her there. Then she went back to her spinning. But before she had more than a few threads spun, the horse, galloping towards the house, threw the stones of the wall down on the pig. Then, trying to get up from where he had fallen down, the horse struck out with his hoofs and killed the pig. When Liban and her mother raised the horse up they found the pig with her head split open. "Every misfortune has come on us since that beggarman came to the house for shelter. He'll want to take our horse now. If he rides away on him I'll be content with my loss, so glad will I be to see the last of the beggarman."

He came back in the evening with his bag as empty as ever. "Where's my pig?" "Our horse killed her." "That horse is mine." "Then take him and ride away, and may our ill-luck go with you." "But I never stay a day less than five days in any house. It's due to a promise that I made to my father. He feared that I might become a vagabond, one day here and another day there, and so he made me promise I'd stay five days in any house I got shelter in.

39

One day more I'll stay for the sake of the promise I made my father. Then I'll away on the horse that I claim from you. I put him in your charge; mind him for me."

The next morning he went off, his bag on his back, and his face towards the crooked lanes of the parish. Liban put a halter on the horse, and, so as not to let him get into any danger, went everywhere the horse wanted to graze. Along the cliff he went, for the grass was sweetest there. When they came to the tree that had the raven's nest in it, Liban put her hand before her eyes so that she might look up and see how high was the tree that the young men were asked to climb. Not so high at all, she thought. And there was the raven on the branch above the nest, flapping her wings at her. As Liban looked, the horse, leaning to get a mouthful of sweet grass, slipped and slithered down the cliff. And the raven with a croak flew down on him.

So poor Liban went back to her mother's house. "Our horse is gone now. Over the cliff he has fallen, and what will the beggarman take from us now?" "Nothing at all can he take," said her mother. "Let him take the horse's skin, and come next nor near us no more."

When he came in that evening the beggarman said, "Where's my horse so that I can go riding to-morrow?" "Under the cliff with the raven upon him, so go now and take his skin and come next my horse when he fell nor near us no more." "Who was minding over the cliff?" "My daughter was minding the horse." "Then your daughter is mine. That's the law, and if you don't think it's the law I'll stand face to face with you about it in the Baron's Court." And saying this the beggarman lifted up Liban (and oh, but his arms were strong!) and thrust her into his bag. Then he put the bag on his back and ran from the house with her.

Her mother ran after him. The neighbors ran with the mother. But the beggarman's legs were long and strong and his back was broad and unbending. "Liban's in the bag, Liban's in the bag—stop him! Stop him!" cried her mother and the neighbors. But their cries only made him go faster and faster. When he came to the cross-roads he laid the bag on a bank and let Liban come out of it.

He had taken off his ragged coat and had washed his face in the stream, and he looked a handsome sort of a young man. "Take me back to my mother," cried Liban. "Here's a coach and we'll go into it," said the young man, and as he spoke a coach with four horses yoked to it drove up. "I'm taking you to claim you in the Baron's Court," said the young man. "My father is the Baron, and when he sees you he'll know I did well to carry you off. There are many things I can do, but there are a few things I can't do, and climbing a tree is one of them. So I put on the beggar's coat and carried this bag on my back to come to you, Liban, Beauty of Woman." Then he put his arms

around her and lifted her into the coach. They were just
in it when Liban's mother and the neighbors came up.
The neighbors stopped to pick up the silver money that
the coachman threw them and the footman lifted Liban's
mother and left her standing beside him at the back of the
coach that went on for a wedding. And as they went on
the Baron's Son sang this song to Liban whose other name
(she had another name) meant Kernel of the Nut:

"HERE'S A COACH AND WE'LL GO INTO IT,"
SAID THE YOUNG MAN.

The hazel in the dell—
A nut with hoarding shell
And sweet and white kernel.

I have for my own,
That nut so tight and brown,
From a branch that I pulled down.

And can take from its shell
The sweet and white kernel—
And that makes all things well!

The bag was mended as the story ended, and Grace handed it to the gentleman, making a curtsy.

"You'll have to let me bestow something on you for doing this for me," he cried, but she shook her head and turned back to the Shoemaker's. And as she did I was made to wonder how a girl who had such brightness about her could live in such a small and tumbled house as Kevin's was. "I have to ask you for something more," said Sir Harry Wildair, "leave to go back with you and take a cup of milk at your door." He went back with her, speaking to her in a low voice, and she kept answering, "only a cup of milk." He stood inside the little porch of the house and I suppose she stayed with him there. He came back slowly and put the shot pheasants in the bag, and went to where the others stood waiting for him. And when I went up to Kevin's house to give the message from my grandmother, Grace was standing there. There was a blush on her face and her lips were closed tightly. "Who can he be, that gentleman?" said I. "Oh, I know who he's not," said she, taking up the besom and sweeping out from the threshold. "He's not the Baron's Son."

WHEN THE BAG WAS MENDED

* * *

THEN a man from the town, the Lawyer's Clerk, came up and spoke to her, and it was plain that it gave him pleasure to spin out his talk with one as fine-looking and as sweet-spoken as the Shoemaker's daughter. Then old Kevin came out with his leather apron on and his big hand grasping the sole of the shoe he was making. The Lawyer's Clerk had an inquiry to make of him, and the two of them went and sat under the Big Tree. I had still to give my grandmother's message to old Kevin, so I went to wait on him beside the Tree while Grace went to do this and that about the little, tumbled house.

THE PEACOCKS OF BARON'S HALL

"THERE is something in the Lease that I copied which surprises me," said the Lawyer's Clerk: "it seems that anyone who takes over Baron's Hall has to keep Peacocks—not any

Peacocks, but the Peacocks that were hatched out in the place. I have been through the grounds and have seen the Peacocks there—Peacocks that are so wild that they roost in the trees—but I never knew before that the owner of Baron's Hall has to keep them there according to Lease." As he talked about the Peacocks and the Lease old Simon the Huntsman came out of the gate of Baron's Hall with his two old hounds beside him; Kevin called to him; the Clerk spoke to him and asked about the Peacocks that were now crying about the Hall. The old Huntsman said:

"This stock of Peacocks has been about the Hall for a hundred years and over a hundred years. Long ago the estate which was a great estate then was owned by one whom the people called The Little Baron. He was only the size of a child of a dozen years, and he had a sister, Lady Sabrina, who was the same size as he was. They were so small, so handsome, and so finely behaved that much was made of them wherever they went. They were in France once and King Louis brought the pair of them to stay in his palace, and when they were leaving he or one of his ladies gave them a Peacock and a Peahen. So the Little Baron and his sister came back to Ireland with the fowl, and they took up their residence in the place that was their father's, in Baron's Hall, which was newly built then, and the Peacock and the Peahen walked upon the lawn, and in a while a clutch of eggs was laid and hatched

THE LAWYER'S CLERK

out and there were Peafowl in numbers parading before the Court.

"That was a long time ago, and the house and lawn were not as they are now, all untidiness and disrepair. It was a very stately place then, and the Peacock and the Peahen that were first there need not have missed the King of France's gardens. The Little Baron and his sister loved to walk where the Peacocks paraded, he in his gold-braided coat with a little sword by his side, and she in her flounces of silks and satins. A picture that is in the gallery shows them walking like that with the Peacocks spreading out their tails for the pair. It was a long time ago, as I have said, and things have changed, and some things have changed for the better. People who kept to the Catholic religion had no right to anything in those days. Well, the Little Baron and his sister belonged to that religion...."

"And in consequence," said the Lawyer's Clerk, "the law did not presume that they owned anything or that they even existed."

"Something like that," said old Simon. "The Little Baron and his sister owned nothing in law. Though everyone agreed that he owned all his fathers had owned the law did not agree. He had no title to possession of anything at all. But his uncles who were not of his religion had the name of owning the estate; it was to them that all rents were paid; it was in their names that everything was bought and sold.

"Well, one day when the Little Baron was walking with Lady Sabrina along where the Peacocks were, their two uncles came to them in their big, heavy riding-boots, their riding-whips in their hands. And as soon as she saw them near her Lady Sabrina drew her arm out of her little brother's arm, and turned to go into the house. Then said brother John or brother Thomas very roughly, 'Enough of such behavior! You must treat us as gentlemen and relatives when we come to visit you!'

"'Nothing,' said she, 'will ever make me acknowledge the presence of men who changed their religion for gain.'

And saying this she walked into the house. She talked like this because she thought of nothing else but her piety. It wasn't the same with her brother—he thought of the grand house he was born in, of the pictures that were in the gallery and of the music that was played for him, and of the Peacocks that paraded where he walked. 'Yes,' cried one of the uncles when Lady Sabrina, drawing up her flounces, went away from the sight of them. 'Yes. But what about these?' And one held up a bag of gold and the other a bag of silver that they carried. 'Here are the rents that your tenants have paid over to us. And if we were not there to receive it in our own names, where would this money go to? Not to where it is going now—into your Steward's counting-house. If the government were not willing to suppose that we are the owners of all that is here, your servants could walk off with your silver and your pictures, your horses and your coaches, and there would be no one to stop them, for you have no title to anything here. Even these Peacocks on the lawn are not yours in the eyes of the law.'

"'We know that,' said the Little Baron, 'and Lady Sabrina and myself live under the protection of the honor of you two. We are in your debt and greatly in your debt, and it is fortunate for us that our father's brothers were not averse to changing their father's religion.'

"'It would have been to Hell or Connaught for you

if we were,' said the brother who was the rougher of the two.

"'Not so harshly, Thomas,' said the other brother.

"'It is as well that those who live in Baron's Hall, who have the horses and the coaches and the servants, know that if we wanted to we and our children could have all this. The estate is ours in the eyes of the law, and all we have to do is to come here and take the benefit of it.'

"'Yes, but men whose fathers were brought up in this house couldn't think of doing such a thing,' said the Little Baron.

"'And we needn't talk about such things,' said brother John. 'Only there will have to be consideration shown to us when we come here. We mustn't be treated as if we were some trooper's sons who have come upon some service to your Lordship. Well, come into the counting-house now and get your Steward to pass on the gold and silver we have brought you.'

"They went into the counting-house, his two uncles and the Little Baron, and the gold and silver was left down, and the Steward set down the sum of it and went through his books to see if it made a balance. Then the Little Baron had his uncles sit down to dinner with him.

"But Lady Sabrina did not come to the table, and when brother John and brother Thomas muttered about this, her brother begged them to excuse her; they knew, he said, that she was pious, and this was the hour, he said, that she went into the chapel. But the uncles did not excuse her; they knew that she would not sit at table with them.

"After dinner brother John and brother Thomas smoked their pipes beside the chimney of the great hall and then made ready to ride to their homes. The Little Baron was not there to see them off. And as they were in their saddles the Steward came up to tell them that there was shortage in the money they had handed him and to blame them for it. This added to the anger that brother John and brother Thomas were in. They had faithfully brought all that should have been given them in rents and here was a servant of the house that their father was born in checking them in this way. They turned upon him and ordered him to bring his master to where they were. But he would not do this: his Lordship, said the Steward, was in his gallery looking at the pictures of vales and groves in France and Italy, and no one was permitted to disturb him. He would report the shortage in the money to him, and that was all he could do about it. He kept on talking about his accounts, but brother John and brother Thomas lashed their horses and galloped down the avenue.

"And when they came to a rise of ground they halted their horses and looked back towards Baron's Hall and saw a little man and a little woman walking on the lawn with Peacocks parading before them, and each said to the other that it was a shame that that estate and that mansion should yield benefit to a pair who thought about pictures and peacocks and chapel-going. For a long time they sat upon their horses and looked over all the properties that they had title to—the fields of barley, oats, and rye with men reaping in them and women lifting up the sheaves, the woods filled with fine timber, the pastures with cattle and horses grazing on them, and then the lake with fishermen's boats upon it. For the first time in their years of guardianship they begrudged these possessions to the Little Baron and became greedy for some of them.

"From that day brother John and brother Thomas began to think of their own advantage as against the Little Baron's. They lost the feeling that the great house their father had come out of should have all their loyalty and all their duty. They thought of the pair who lived there as odd little strangers who were always making claims upon them, always holding them at fault. They began to put to their own use part of the rents that came into their hands for the Little Baron. And when the Steward demanded an accounting from them they threw him into the bed of nettles outside his countinghouse and rode away. Then they made great outlays with the money paid to them for the Lord in Baron's Hall: brother John bought a herd of fine cattle for his pasture, and brother Thomas bought the best of racers and hunters for his stables. A time came when they brought no money at all into the counting-house. Their cheating went on and the years went by. And brother John and brother Thomas, knowing they had dishonored their name, spent days in drinking and nights in gambling. They took the Little Baron's horses out of his stables, and they put their own fishermen upon his lake.

"They needed more and more money. Then there came an officer from England who wanted timber for the King's ships, and he offered them a thousand pounds for the woods that were around Baron's Hall. The brothers took the money and sent men to cut the trees and cart the timbers away. The Little Baron was upon the lawn with his sister, and the Peacocks, now become a great flock, were parading before him, when the news was brought to him that the woods were being cut down. He and Lady Sabrina mounted their ponies and rode to where the axes were sounding. Many fine trees were already on the ground. Standing up in his stirrups the Little Baron ordered the wood-cutters to stop, and they, knowing what rights he had there, let the axes lie. But his uncles came forward and told the men to take their order from those who had title to the woods, and told him that whether he liked it or not the woods would go down. The little man upon the pony denounced them for their faithlessness, and they turned from him as from an ungovernable child and bade the men who were near it to chop the branches off a tree that had fallen down some time before.

"Its trunk lay over a wall that its fall had broken down and its roots were above a pit they had been dragged out of. These roots with the clay on them stood up like a mound and in a hollow amongst them a wren had built her nest. Young ones were in it; they were nearly ready to fly, and the mother, frightened at the sound and the shaking of the earth where her nest was, flew to them and away from them and back to them again. The cutting off of the branches would make the butt of the tree settle back into the pit again and crush the nest and the birds. Lady Sabrina saw this and she asked that the tree be left as it was until the wrens flew away. But the uncles would not have the men stop; there was nothing else for them to do with the light axes they had, and they must keep on working for their penny a day. The branches were cut off, the butt of the tree was slipping down when the little lady sprang into the pit and tore the nest out of its hollow. But what could she do with it? She left it on the ground and sitting down beside it broke into crying. The wren passed under her hand into and out of the nest.

"Then her brother took her hand and led her away. The two little people walked beside the ponies that the grooms led back to the Hall, and the men were ordered to bend their backs to the work.

"When he went home the Little Baron sat down and wrote letters to the gentlemen of the county informing them of his uncles' behavior to him. Many of the gentlemen refused to speak to or to recognize brother John or brother Thomas after that. But this was no help to the Little Baron's cause. For as the finer gentlemen fell away from them, the gentlemen whose rebuke might have mattered to them, the uncles took up more and more with men who, coming from menial ranks, had profited by the overturn of the old nobility. These men as they sat with brother John and brother Thomas and drank with them or played cards with them laughed at them for not taking possession of Baron's Hall and all that was in it and around it.

"Then, after a night at the gaming-table, with their clothes disordered and their faces heavy, his two uncles rode up to the front of the Little Baron's house and sent in a message that they were bringing the High Sheriff to visit him. They tramped up the stairway and they went into the room where the Little Baron was lying on his wide bed. The High Sheriff told him that the owners of Baron's Hall were about to take possession of it and of the whole of the estate. It must have been that the Little Baron had expected some such visitation, for he raised himself in his bed and said to them very coolly, 'Who said that I am not as well able to change my religion as others of my family?' And when he said that the heavy faces of brother John and brother Thomas became white and they drew away to talk together. For if he changed his religion he would gain title to his possessions and his uncles would be cast off from his estate. 'Who said I could not change my religion like others of my family?' They heard him say the words over again to the High Sheriff, and they went out of the room and waited before the door. 'You have three days to come to me and take the test that will show you have come over to the King's religion,' the High Sheriff said. 'Three days—that is very well,' said the Little Baron, and he rose from his bed and dressed himself, and to be courteous to the High Sheriff, who was himself a lord's son, he took him through the gallery and showed him his pictures of vales in France and groves in Italy. And by the time he brought him to the doorway, brother John and brother Thomas had ridden away.

"That evening they sat by their chimney, strong drink beside them, thinking they had been ill-counseled to go as far as they had gone. For if the Lord of Baron's Hall changed, in spite of his sister's prayers, his religion, he would have title to his estate and the law would be by him. They would have nothing then—they would be men without place or fortune. Moreover, the Little

Baron might be able to bring them to trial for some of the heedless things they had done, and make them fly the country, or see the inside of a prison. In three days they might be—they would be, they thought—at the mercy of the Little Baron.

"And the Little Baron saw the sunlight on the turrets of his stately house and on the woods that were still around it, and he saw his Peacocks parading upon the lawn, and he thought that the only life that could give him pleasure and content was here, and that if he gave it up he would be mournful and complaining for the rest of his days—he would grow old as a feeble and banished creature. His sister prayed in the chapel that he might not forsake his religion, but he knew that the belief that made her pray so fervently was not in him. He had only to say that this belief was no longer his and he would have riches and the secure life that he and his sister needed more than any other man and woman. And the men who had humbled and tormented him would be at his mercy. He thought of all this walking up and down there, and then with the firm tread of a man who has a right to carry a sword he went to where his sister was kneeling. 'What have you come to say to me?' she asked, raising up her little figure to stand beside his little figure. 'We belong,' said he, 'to the nobility of the Gael and the Sean-ghaill— to the MacMahons and the Fitz-urses, and it is not for us to change our creed for riches and security. I who am rightfully the heir to that name and this place can say nothing else.' He gave his arm to his sister then, and they went upstairs and downstairs telling the servants that the house would be in their possession for only a while longer; then one went into her chapel and the other into his gallery, and they prepared for the leave-taking that had to be.

"When the High Sheriff came he found them watching their Peacocks upon the lawn. The Little Baron led him into the house; the test that might be offered him he could not take, he said. Then he had his Steward deliver to the High Sheriff all the papers that had to do with the family and the estate, and he gave his arm to his sister, and the two walked down the avenue of elm trees, while the servants who had been forbidden to make any clamor stood to watch them, and the bell that was in the yard one pulled at and it rang very mournfully.

"Brother John and brother Thomas were outside the gate; they stood aside as the pair passed them. One and then another of the Peacocks cried. 'Do not scatter my Peacocks,' said the Little Baron to brother John. And the man made a sign of promise.

"The Little Baron and Lady Sabrina went to live in a lodge that was on a hill above this place; it had a sort of turret, and every day he and his sister would mount up and look across the wall and upon the lawn of Baron's Hall. They could see the Peacocks there and they would spend a long time watching them, and as they watched them they would remind each other of the court of the King of France and of the fountains and gardens and the stately life that was there. Their uncles with their families had taken possession of Baron's Hall, and the place was losing its stately appearance. More and more of the trees were cut down; the gardens became wilder and the lawn grew rougher. The lovely things that were within the house were taken away—brother John sold the pictures of vales in France and groves in Italy to give a dowry to his daughter. But he would not have the flock of Peacocks scattered—they went upon the lawn, more and more of them.

"The uncles died, and the son of one of them came into the ownership of Baron's Hall. This man, too, let the Peacocks remain unscattered. But now the wildness they grew up in lessened the broods—the weasel got many of the young ones. The gold lace raveled off the Little Baron's coat and the silks and satins that went into the flounces of his sister's dresses wore out. They became so poor that oftentimes there was no candle to light their chamber in the winter nights. But withal they remained a stately pair, and they would never take anything from the Lord of Baron's Hall.

"They died in the lodge there, one going soon after the other. The Little Baron, dying first, was buried in the grounds of Baron's Hall. His sister asked that she be buried beside him, and the ground was consecrated for her burial. I can show you where the graves are—there where there are three dark yew trees. Things have changed very much since they were buried there, and Baron's Hall is no more than a ruin now. But the Peacocks are still there, and, as the people will tell you, there is never a season when a wren may not be seen fluttering about the ground where the dark yew trees are. Many owners of the Hall have come and gone since, but all of them left it in their wills that the Peacocks were not to be banished. Aye, and when the last of the family leased the place to other people it was put into the lease that they were to be kept there."

"I copied that clause out," said the Lawyer's Clerk. "I was much surprised by it."

"At some time of the year," said the old Huntsman, "the Peacocks fly up into the branches of the yew trees and they can be heard crying all together."

THE SHOEMAKER

* * *

OUR Cobbler had a saying which I heard from him often enough. "Well, these may be Nannie's shoes." He'd say this as he'd take up a pair belonging to some little girl; no matter who else might be waiting to have boots or shoes repaired by him, these would be the ones that he would put the first stitch into or the first bit on. "These may be Nannie's shoes." There really was a child named Nannie: she lived in the place that Kevin had come from—our Kevin the Cobbler. She had left a pair of brown shoes with him, wanting to have them mended for Sunday. Well, Kevin got engaged in mending a big pair of fishing-boots for the lord of the place, and when Nannie came to fetch hers they were just as she had left them. She gave him such a mournful look that Kevin never forgot it; no matter who had to wait he would repair the shoes that had been left him by this or that little girl afterwards. "They may be Nannie's shoes," he would say, and leave everything else aside until he had mended them.

There he was under the Tree, and beside him was his bench with all the things on it that you see on cobblers' benches the world over—a little bowl with wax in it; a tobacco-box filled with little nails; scraps of leather; awls; blades of different kinds and sizes; more nails; and, very surprisingly, in the middle of all these unusual things, the pipe we were used to seeing in his mouth or his hand. I had left my boots with him to be mended, and although I was glad to be going about in my bare feet this summer's day, I wanted to have boots on my feet on Sunday, and Kevin was to put soles and heels on them. Near him was a basket in which were the boots he was to repair—I could name the boys and girls they all belonged to—Joe's boots and Ellen's, Winnie's and Jimmie's, Peter's and Nora's. And there was the Cobbler with his leather apron on, pulling the waxed thread through a patch, or smoothing a heel with his ball, or spanning a heel and toe with his big hand. My boots were near to his hand, and I said, "You'll do mine next, won't you?" But Kevin took up a pair belonging to a little girl, and he said, "These may be Nannie's shoes, and I'll have to do them first." I sat down and watched him work with his needle and his little stumpy knife this or that piece of leather that would just cover the break in a boot. "And where did Nannie get the

KEVIN THE COBBLER

shoes she brought to you?" I asked him. "I will tell you that," said Kevin, and as he bent his head over the sole of the shoe, stitching it and tapping it, he told me the story of:

NANNIE'S SHOES

THE house that Nannie and her mother lived in stood by itself. It was a very little house, and so low that the tall weed that grew beside the door was nearly up to the roof. The wings of the sea-gulls looked very big when they spread over that house, Nannie often thought. It stood near where the fishing-boats came in. Her mother earned a living by doing different things—laundry-work, and knitting, and sewing. But she earned it mainly by selling fish—herring and mackerel—at houses that were a couple of miles away. She would get two baskets of fish from a boat, and, carrying them on her arms, would go off, twice a week, and sell them.

When Nannie came into the house one day she had something surprising to tell. She told it, and her mother, taking the herrings that were left in the basket, scraped the bright scales off, cleaned them and sprinkled flour on them, and left them ready for cooking. Then Nannie, having lighted the fire, washed the potatoes and put them on to boil. What she had to tell was that she was to be confirmed in May. "It's strange to me that you are so much grown. I didn't think it was so long since you were born," her mother said. The day she would be confirmed would be her birthday—she would be ten that day. Nannie, as she watched the potatoes cooking, thought how different they were from yesterday, the days that were before her until May.

She was younger than the others who were to be confirmed by the Bishop. But she knew her catechism very well and could repeat long prayers that the others didn't know. So she was put into the class that was being prepared for confirmation. Then she heard the others tell about the dresses they would wear on that grand day—white muslin dresses. Hers wouldn't be different; her mother had yards of muslin to make a summer-dress for her, and so Nannie would be as fine as any of the others. But when she heard some of them tell how they would wear brown shoes with their white dresses, Nannie's heart sank down; what she had to wear on her feet were boots—heavy, awkward boots. They would show below her muslin dress, these boots that could hardly be polished, and when she walked in procession, no one would notice her muslin dress, for everyone would be looking at her ugly, heavy boots.

Nannie remembered all the pairs she had had in her lifetime. They weren't so many. In the summer she ran around in her bare feet, and that meant that a pair of boots, with many mendings, lasted her from Christmas to Christmas. She had had a pair that proved to be a very bad bargain; they wore out at Easter. Then her mother had bought her shoes—she called them shoes because they were low and light—which she could wear until the summer came in and then wear again until Christmas. She had thought that these shoes were lovely. There were no rows of broad nails on their soles to make them wear longer; she could go with great ease in them; they were brown. Her mother had said that when summer was over she would buy her a pair of boots; then she would have a pair of boots and a pair of shoes, and she could wear her shoes on a Sunday. But when summer was over her mother had less shillings than ever, and Nannie had to wear her brown shoes until her toes came through the soles; she got chilblains, and by the time she was able to go about in her bare feet, her lovely brown shoes were broken and all out of shape. No cobbler could do anything to fix them. When summer was over she got a pair of boots, and these she was wearing now; there were rows of nails on their soles which made them very heavy, and, no matter how much she scraped and rubbed them the leather would not take a real shine; these boots never looked polished.

Now her mother said, "I can make a white dress for you and I can buy nice ribbons for you, and you'll look as well as any of the others." "Isn't it a pity," said Nannie, "that my brown shoes are worn out—they'd have been so nice with my muslin dress and all the others are going to wear brown shoes." Her mother said something that was very hopeful. "Please God, before May, I'll have shillings enough to buy brown shoes for you."

After they had eaten their dinner they went outside: Nannie's mother was spreading on the stones the clothes she had taken out of the wash-tub, and Nannie sat thinking of all she would have to know before confirmation day.

"I'll have to know a lot of things," said she to her mother, "and you'll have to tell me." "What sort of things?" her mother asked quickly. "About God, and why we were made," said Nannie. And then the question she was longing to ask came upon the tip of her tongue, and she said, "Will my father ever come to us here?" Her mother had a big pebble in her hand. She threw it away as if she were throwing it at someone. She said, "No, Nannie, he will never come to us here."

The next week the boats came in with hardly any herrings. Then they were so dear that the people in the village did not buy from Nannie's mother. The week after the catches were so big that there was hardly anything to be made by carrying a few baskets of them to the houses—cart-loads were brought up there. And so it got near to May and Nannie's mother hadn't the extra shillings that she thought she would have for the purchase of the brown shoes. She got no more knitting or sewing to do. Nannie got very downhearted and brought out her broken shoes and tried to fix them into some shape. And when her mother saw her doing this, she said, "I'll do what I never thought I should do. I'll send you to the house at the cross-roads to ask the Johnsons to give me the knitting they want done."

Nannie knew that house at the cross-roads. When she passed by it she felt the same as when she passed by a churchyard. And she didn't know why she felt like this. Once when she was very little and walking along the road with her mother, they met the old woman Johnson, and she had taken down the shawl that was about Nannie's head, and, looking her full in the face, had said to her mother, "So this is the child? But I want you to know that it is nothing to me that you say so." Nannie had always remembered the woman who had looked at her in this judging and grudging way. Someone who was with her when she was passing the house another time told her that the Johnsons had had a son, a young man named Michael, who was drowned when a boat was overturned in a storm. Now there was no one with them; there were only the old man and the old woman living together in the house at the cross-roads. Nannie thought that this house was, maybe, haunted—haunted by the young man who was drowned—and that this accounted for her being so fearful when she went near it.

"I'll send you to the house at the cross-roads." But her mother did not do this for a few days longer. Then when Nannie talked to her very anxiously about the prospect of buying the shoes, her mother said to her, "Go now and ask them to give me the knitting they want done. But they'll be very surprised at your coming to them on such an errand."

And now she was on her way to that house. When

she came to the cross-roads she did not go to the house at once; her mother had told her that she was not to let anyone see her going into the Johnsons'. So she waited in the twilight. She waited until the candle was lighted in the window; night had come and it would not do for her to stay out too late. She rapped at the door; her heart beat loudly as she waited. Someone came to open the door. It was the old man. He stood peering at her for a long time, and she wasn't able to speak to him. "My mother sent me..." she said, and without speaking to her he caught her arm and brought her within.

It was a very wide room she was brought into, with beams across the ceiling and flags upon the floor, and a high clock that went ticking, ticking. There was a white cat before the fire and there was an old woman seated on a bench. "This is the child," said the man. "What does she want?" said the old woman, rising up. "What have you come for?" she said, drawing Nannie to her.

"My mother told me to say, ma'am, that she would do work for you—knitting work."

"What else did she say?"

"Nothing else at all, ma'am."

The old man had seated himself at the fire and was looking full at her. But the way he looked at her was nothing to the way the old woman looked at her. She looked at her so hard that Nannie thought she was looking through her. And then she looked at her forehead and her hair, her eyes and nose and mouth and chin.

"What do you do?" she said.

"I learn my catechism and I am preparing to be confirmed," said Nannie. The Johnsons, she knew, were of a different religion from herself and her mother, and she didn't know but what she said might make them cross.

"When will your confirmation be?"

"In May, ma'am."

"I didn't think it was so long since you were born," said the old woman. Nannie was surprised to hear her say just what her own mother had said. What was it to this old woman seated at the fire in the house at the cross-roads when she was born, and how much she had grown, and how soon she was to be confirmed?

"We needn't talk to the child about that," said the old man. "Do you want to give the woman any knitting to do?"

"If she does anything for me I'll pay her the price and nothing over the price," said the old woman.

"Well, will you give her the knitting to do?"

"I don't know that I will." Nannie's heart sank. After her venturing into this place she wouldn't get her brown shoes, after all, maybe.

"Why did she send you to ask this of me?"

"My mother would like me to have brown shoes on

my feet when I'm getting confirmed—the other girls all will have them," said Nannie.

"What about the yarn you bought on St. Martin's Day?" said the old man to his wife. "You haven't done anything with it since."

"I may do something with it when the days get longer and I'm able to see better," said the old woman. Nannie knew that the old man would be glad to help her mother, but the old woman didn't want any kindness to be between them.

"I think the child is certainly like..." said he.

"You needn't say who she's like," said the old woman. "Anyway, it does me no good to see her."

"It would be no harm to let her knit what you were going to knit," said the old man. And then he said after a while, "It will do no harm to let her have the yarn."

"No harm if she knows that she will get only the price that anyone else would get from me."

"She knows that—she can't help but know that," said the old man.

Then the old woman went to the press and took out hanks of yarn. Oh, very blue was that yarn, and very soft as Nannie felt when it was put into her arms. "Tell your mother to make a shawl for me—she used to be good at knitting a shawl. I will buy the shoes for you and they'll

be here when you bring the shawl to me." Then she bade
Nannie sit on a stool before where the cat was and take
her heavy boots off; the old man measured the soles of her
feet. "What kind of shoes do you want?" he asked her.

"Brown shoes," Nannie whispered.

"Well, they'll be here for you when you bring the
shawl," the old man said. Then Nannie rose to go. "Stay
and warm yourself," he said.

So Nannie sat at the Johnsons' fire and looked at a
ship that was on the mantelpiece until she saw it inside
herself as well as outside herself. The clock ticked and
ticked and the old man and woman kept their eyes on her.
At last he told her she could be going home, and she stood
up and he opened the door for her and she went out holding the yarn in her arms. She stopped to fasten a boot that
had not been tied, and she heard the old man say before
he closed the door, "She's Michael's child indeed," and
she heard the old woman say in such a crying voice that
she was sorry for her, hard and all as she was, "My child,
Michael." Then Nannie went down the road knowing
that the man who was drowned out of that house was
her father, and that it was likely he was drowned because
the old woman did not want him to be friends with her
mother. Maybe he was going to do something for her
mother, or get help for her when he was drowned. But
she only thought of this while she went a little piece of the

road, for the people in the house at the cross-roads were far from her mind, and she had no notion of what the man who was drowned was like. And so as she went the greater part of the road holding the light and soft hanks of yarn she was thinking of the brown shoes she would be able to wear with her muslin dress.

She told her mother what she had heard said and told her nothing of the thought she had had. She held the blue yarn stretched on her arms while her mother wound it into a blue ball, and then she went to bed.

She got up with something grand to think about— the brown shoes that would surely be hers and that she could wear on Sundays after the confirmation, wearing her boots on week-days. Next evening she stood holding a second hank of yarn which her mother was winding into a second ball. "They're not thinking about you, or whether or not you are grown," her mother said when she repeated again the sayings of the old man and woman. "They are thinking about a man who was drowned when you were born—that very day." "I know that," said Nannie. "They called him Michael." "And do you know who he was?" "Yes," Nannie whispered. "You are my mother and he was my father." "That is the truth." Her mother said no more, and when that hank of yarn was wound she let Nannie go to sit under where the candle was lighted and go over the page of catechism she had to learn. "What is Man?" her mother asked, asking the question whose answer Nannie had to know. "Man," repeated Nannie, "is a creature composed of a body and soul and made in God's likeness." "It's hard to understand," said her mother, "how the soul can be in a far place and here with us, too, when the body's drowned. It can be near us, Nannie." "And it can be near them, too," said Nannie, "them at the cross-roads."

Her mother, when she returned with baskets emptied or not altogether emptied, and when she had washed and ironed, and when Nannie, home from school, had cooked what there was to be cooked, stayed outside as long as daylight lasted, knitting with her two bone needles and making blue worsted into bigger and bigger squares of shawl. And when it would come windy outside she would stand beside the little window within, knitting away and not speaking until the time came for Nannie to put the pot over the fire, and watch and stir it until the porridge bubbled up, sitting with the catechism on her lap, repeating the questions and the answers.

Working under the light of the candle, her mother finished the shawl one night and put fringes on it. It was the loveliest blue shawl Nannie had ever seen, and her mother thought that it was the best she had ever knit. The same evening Nannie had by heart the last of the questions and answers she had to know. And next day, when she was coming from school, she saw the old man and the old woman; they were traveling back from the town in their cart, and Nannie knew that they had her brown shoes with them. She longed to take the shawl and go with it to the house at the cross-roads that evening, and get the shoes, and to have them a day sooner and a day longer than she had expected to have them. But her mother wouldn't have her go out that night.

Happily she wakened up with the thought that the shawl was made and that the brown shoes were being kept for her. She put the shawl over her when she was dressed, and saw how blue it was and felt how soft it was. Then she went to school. No longer did she fear to have questions out of the catechism asked her—she knew every answer. No longer did she feel down-hearted when she heard the others talk about the shoes they would wear; now she was able to speak up and tell them about her muslin dress and brown shoes.

The door of the house was shut when she came home from school; her mother was not at home, and this surprised Nannie, for it was not her day to go with the fish to the village. She could not think where her mother could be. She waited a long time before the closed door, wondering what could have happened to keep her away so long, and she was nearly worn away with anxiety when her mother appeared. She was carrying a basket and as soon as they were within, she took out of the basket, not cabbages that Nannie thought were in it, but her dress— her muslin dress, whole, finished, and ready to wear. Her mother had been in a place where she could look at the sea, and there she had finished the making of the dress. Nannie was to put it on as soon as she had eaten her dinner, and go to the house at the cross-roads wearing it.

Her mother folded up the shawl and gave it to her to carry. She went quickly to the cross-roads. The candle was not yet lighted in the window, and when she knocked the old man came slowly across the kitchen and opened the door to her. The old woman was not there; she was outside in the hen-yard.

The old man bade her put the shawl around her, so that, as he said, he could see how it hung. Nannie, very shyly, did as she was asked. She was standing there with the blue shawl around her, and the old man, the candle he had lighted in his hand, looking at her, when the old woman came in by the back door. Immediately Nannie took the shawl and gave it to her. "Blue goes well with her black hair and gray eyes," said the old man.

She sat at the fire, and the pair looked at her as if they were searching for something in her face; the shawl was on the old woman's lap. "Take off your boots," the old man said to her.

Sitting on the stool, she took her boots off; the old

man put the brown shoes on her feet. She stood up, and oh, how light they were! How lovely they looked below her muslin dress!

"Thank you, ma'am," said Nannie to the old woman.

"You have nothing to thank me for—the making of the shawl is full value for the shoes. Mind, I don't want to give you anything."

"No, ma'am."

"Put your boots on again and wear them going down the muddy bit of road."

"Yes, ma'am."

Nannie put on her boots and took the brown shoes under her arm. She went down the road. She began to hurry, thinking how far away was the house in which she would show her mother the shoes on her feet and spend a long time herself looking at them. Yes, the house was far away, but when she got to that bush it would be nearer. So she hurried towards the bush. She heard a voice behind her and stopped, her heart beating. The old man was hurrying after her. Was it to take back the shoes? He came beside her. He held something towards her—the shawl. Yes, that was it; there was something that wasn't finished, and because of that she wouldn't be allowed to take the shoes away, and she mightn't have them, after all, for her confirmation. She stood holding the shoes tightly clasped and ready to cry. "Take the shawl—you can have it for

yourself," said the old man. "Herself wishes you to have
it. She'll get your mother to make another for her—a red
shawl the same as she's used to wearing. The blue one
became you well; she saw you with it on you, and when
you were out of the house she said that Michael had hair
like yours and your kind of eyes, and she'd like you to
wear it on the day that will be the day he was drowned.
The blue of the shawl brought that out. He had hair
like yours and your kind of eyes, and she's not a hard old
woman, though she never could like your mother. Here's
the shawl for you. She was mad with Michael for liking
your mother—that was the way it was with her. But she
wanted you to have the blue shawl, Nannie."

He was gone back to the house. Then the distance
between bush and bush seemed even greater to Nannie
as she ran along. How long it would be before she could
show herself to her mother, not only with her brown
shoes on, but with the blue shawl around her! And then
she was standing in the middle of the room with her muslin dress on, and her brown shoes, and the blue shawl
across her shoulders, and her mother was looking at her
with her eyes very bright and saying that there should be
another to look at her and to see how fine and handsome
she was.

In a week she went to confirmation. Her muslin dress
was on her and her brown shoes, and as the day was a

little windy, she wore the blue knitted shawl around her shoulders, but not so as to hide any of the muslin dress. Her brown shoes were admired by all. The grown people said, "How nice it is to see that that poor child has had such good rearing and good care. She is as well dressed and she carries herself as well as if she had a father who owned all the boats in the bay."

YOU'VE BEEN TO THE CIRCUS

* * *

YOU were at the Circus and now you want me, as we sit under the Big Tree, to tell you histories of Clowns and Riders and Acrobats and Circus-horses. You tell me everything that was done and said....It surely was very droll and very lively. Have you no more to tell me? Well, then, I'll tell you this very sober history. Nobody ever told it to me, and if you ask me how I got to know it I'll have to tell you that a little bird on whose tail I put some salt told it to me. I'll name my history:

THE THREE COMPANIONS

ANYONE could know that William was a Circus-horse, and anybody could know that he was too old to be a bargain for anyone except, maybe, the Knacker. The bit of mane that he had straggled down in strings, his stump of tail was unlifted, and his head was hanging.

His ribs and knees and shoulder-bones were all showing.
He had color, but you couldn't be sure whether it was
dark with patches of gray on it, or gray with patches of
dark. William went along the road as if he were trying to
remember something, and that was what he was doing.
He believed in improving his mind, and the way he used
to improve it was by repeating, when he was alone, the
names of the rivers of Ireland. He knew quite a number
of them and had given himself the habit of saying them
over when he had nothing else to think about. But try as
he would he could remember no more than two of them
as he went along the road by himself, pulling a bit of grass
out of the ditches. "The Moy, the Suck...." He felt that
he was getting very feeble in his mind.

He stumbled against a Donkey. She got up quickly
from where she was lying and stood beside William.
After a while he said to her, "Where do we go?" It was
a natural question for a Circus-horse to ask, for they are
always going somewhere.

"I hadn't thought about going anywhere," said the
Donkey. Her name was Kate Ann, and she was commonly
called "Git-on" for she belonged to an Apple-woman and
used to draw the cart with the apples piled on it, and
stand all day beside it while the old woman sold apples
at a ha'penny each to the boys who had a ha'penny. But
times had got bad, and the old woman hadn't money to

buy apples, and as she couldn't buy them she couldn't sell them, and so she had taken the harness off Kate Ann's back and had allowed her to go where she could pick up a mouthful of grass.

"I don't know where we might go," said she to William.

A Goat that had jumped up at the other side of the fence came down where the pair were standing. "We'll follow him," said the Donkey. When a Goat walks on looking as if he knew where he was going a Horse or a Donkey can hardly help but follow him. And this Goat looked as if he knew where he was going and a lot besides. He belonged to a Lodge of Loyal and Independent Men. He heard their speeches at the Lodge meetings and he marched in their parades to the beating of the drum, his horns decked with the ribbons of the Order. These ribbons were on them now, for the parading Lodge had only just lost him. What made this Goat (Billy was his name) so sure of himself was that he was able to say:

> *I am an Independent Man*
> *From Portadown upon the Bann.*

And also:

The crown of the causeway on roadway and street,
And the Teagues under my feet.

"Come on," he said, as if he knew that the others wanted to follow him. "Come on," he said, speaking like the Grand Master of the Order. He led them towards the hills, eating a tuft of grass here and a tuft of grass there, with William and Kate Ann drinking out of the little pools by the way.

This story is about these three, but it is principally about William. A cart with a quick mare between the shafts had come towards Bunlahy. Two were seated in front, and one on a very shaky seat was at the tail-end of the cart. This one was holding a rope which led a horse that was striving to keep up with the cart.

Just as they had arrived here the led horse stopped; the rope dragged him on, but then he spread out his feet and wouldn't go a bit farther. The man on the shaky seat had jumped off the cart. He had done his jump surprisingly well and he stood facing the animal. The cart with the fast mare between its shafts hadn't stopped at all, but had gone faster and faster towards the brown bogs of Monamore.

The man had a long and loose coat on him and his hat was a very queer one—it was high in the crown and it had hardly any brim. His long face had knobs all over it; he had no eyebrows and his eyes were very quiet. "So you won't come, William?" he said. "Well, you're wise not to come." Holding the rope in his hand he had bowed towards the Big Tree under which nobody was seated. "I am Bob Cinnamon the Circus-clown," he had said, "and this is William, my steed. The Circus is broken up; the riders have enlisted in the Militia, and the Ring-master has been put in the Lockup. All that belongs to me is my steed. But William is too aged a horse to be worth anything to me alive. There should be something for his hide, something for his hoofs that can be melted down into glue. I was taking him to the Knacker's Yard to sell the old works. But he won't let himself be brought there, it appears. Well, go your own way, William, my steed, and may your luck be the best." So Cinnamon the Clown had taken the halter off his neck and had left him standing by the Big Tree. Going into Mrs. Dunphy's he had bought a penny roll for himself and had then walked on and out of sight, his hands in the pockets of his long, loose coat.

And that is how William had come to the place where he had met Kate Ann first and Billy afterwards. They had gone towards the hills, as I have told you. They came to a gateway before a big house, and Billy boldly led them up the avenue to it. Now this was a house that something was happening in. The master had gone away leaving it in charge of his steward and his bailiff, and that was to his loss, for these fellows had taken away the horses and the cattle and had brought robbers in to help them to plunder the house. The robbers were there when the Horse, the Goat, and the Donkey came before the house. They were sitting at a table, dividing the candlesticks and spoons, and putting the silver money in a bag; the steward and the bailiff were claiming their shares from the robbers. At that very minute, Billy, having marched up to it, struck the doors with his horns. Kate Ann threw back her head and said, "Haw-haw-haw-haw." And William the Circus-horse stood upon his hind-legs making a queer sound as he walked around, and then a great clatter as he struck the cobbles with his forefeet. When the knocking and the braying and the clattering were heard at the table the fellows thought that the justices were coming in on them, and they grabbed the candlesticks and the spoons and the bag of silver money, ran down the back passages, jumped out of the window, and hied them through the plantation and away down to the roadway. That doesn't take them out of the story, however. Going along the road in the dark of the night, the steward and bailiff and the robbers met the procession of Loyal and Independent Men who had suffered the loss of Billy, their Goat, and they got beaten with drumsticks and flutes, and the one who was carrying it let the silver money spill out of the bag and into the grass on the roadway. Bob Cinnamon the Clown

THE FELLOWS THOUGHT THAT THE JUSTICES WERE
COMING IN ON THEM.

came that way next morning; he picked up enough silver
money to fill the pockets of his long, loose coat.

As for the Horse, the Donkey, and the Goat, they
went into the stable out of which the horses had been stolen, and found the place very warm and pleasant. Indeed,
neither William nor Kate Ann had ever been in such
comfortable quarters before, and Billy, used as he was to
good lodgings, thought that the place was as right as could
be. William slept there as a horse sleeps—he only knows
when he sleeps that he is not moving; Kate Ann slept as

a donkey sleeps that always expects to be made get up and carry something; Billy slept as a goat sleeps that can hardly be said to sleep at all because he is so anxious to be going somewhere.

When morning came Billy marched out of the stable, singing:

I am an Independent Man
From Portadown upon the Bann.

William and Kate Ann went after him. They found no one about the place. A smell of cabbages came to Billy, and he marched through a gate and into a garden. He was astounded at the sight that met his eyes. He thought for a while he was surely dreaming, for here were cabbages, not in half-dozens and dozens, but in rows and rows—cabbages with curly leaves, cabbages with smooth leaves and white heads inside them, and cabbages of a rare, purplish color. They were all spreading themselves out and crying, "Eat me, eat me!" Billy went into the middle of the garden and began to eat to the right and the left, and each leaf he ate seemed sweeter than the other. He ate more than twenty cabbages, and then he went and lay down where wild cabbages with yellow flowers were growing and watched the clouds go by.

And never had an Apple-woman's Donkey so many

carrots under her nose as Kate Ann had when she went into a shed that she found a good smell coming out of. There were baskets and baskets of carrots there. She bit into one and the taste was delightful; she munched it and expected someone to come and drive her out of the shed before she had eaten it all. But no one came in. She ate it and then ate another. Still no one came and Kate Ann ate all the carrots that were in one of the baskets. Then she went outside and found William standing before a rick of hay. "Do you see what I see?" he said to her. "I see more hay than ever I saw in all the days of my life," said Kate Ann to him. "Well, if you can see it, I can eat it," said William, "but I thought that I was dreaming." He ate out of the rick until he was satisfied and well satisfied. He knew now that he had been hungry for years—hungry for just the sort of hay that was in the rick he had come to. Kate Ann would have eaten out of the same rick only she had had her fill of carrots.

Now William stood before the door of the house, and Kate Ann and Billy stood beside him. What sort of a place was this, they wondered, where there were such good things to be had without any man doing anything to upset their enjoyment of them? And then a tame Magpie hopped out of the hall, and, perching on one of the house-steps, told them what had happened in the house.

William went into the hall and climbed the first flight

of stairs. He had to come down backwards, however. He saw a table in the hall with a bell on it and a chair before it. He sat down on the chair and took up the bell with his forefeet and rang it. Billy and Kate Ann were so surprised at this turn that they could only say "ma-ah" and "haw-haw." When they recovered they told him that he was the most wonderful being that ever went on four legs. William was very modest about his performance, and assured them that if they had belonged to a circus they could have seen things that were just as remarkable.

But the Magpie that was perched at the head of the stairway didn't like the bell-ringing at all. It meant that one of the animals that had come to the house had an accomplishment, and no one, the Magpie thought, thought, should have an accomplishment but herself: she could talk men's language—that was hers. She got very cross at what she saw William doing, and there and then she made up her mind that she would get the three companions away from the manor.

In the evening the three went into the stable, closing the door behind them. Such was their good-fellowship that they told each other all the things they knew. Billy spoke about Lodge-meetings and Parades and Processions, and his two companions were astonished to hear of such goings-on. William could remember ten of the names of the rivers of Ireland, beginning, "The Barrow, the Suit, the Nore," and he told them to Kate Ann. She tried to remember a song that began: *At six o'clock in the morning at the Cabbage-market gate...*

She could only remember the first line, but she knew the tune very well and beat it out on the pavement with her forefeet. They went to sleep in their different ways, and as soon as light came they left the stable. Billy went into the cabbage-garden, Kate Ann into the shed where the baskets of carrots were, and William to the rick of hay. They found themselves even more refreshed than they were the day before. As a signal for them to get ready to go for a stroll William went into the hall and rang the bell. Then they went up the hillside, Billy leading. Kate Ann talked to them about apples, and Billy, who knew the taste of apples, put in a word now and again. They did not know that the Magpie was planning to separate them and get them away from the manor.

They had a restful evening; in the morning each went to his and her good meal; each felt even in better spirits than on the day before. But now the Magpie was ready with her plan. She flew up on a currant-bush that Billy was lying under while he watched the clouds go by. "Your friends, the Donkey and the Horse, have been talking about you," she said to him. "I overheard what they said. They want to get rid of you because they think you're too domineering—you are that, you know. You'd be surprised to hear what the Donkey told the Horse to do about you." "What did he tell him to do?" asked Billy, who was easily aroused to believe that designs against him were being formed. "You'd be surprised—I know you'd be surprised," said the Magpie. "Tell me what they said or get out of this," said Billy, who was getting angrier and angrier. "Well, if you must know," said the Magpie, "they're going to send for the Policemen, and that means the lock-up for you, Billy, my lad, on a charge of cabbage-stealing." And when she had said this, the Magpie flew away.

She flew over to where William and Kate Ann were standing together; both were enjoying the quietude of the day and the feeling they had that no one was going to trouble them. The Magpie lighted on a gate-post. "Here you are," said she, "and no one would think that you had any reason to be afraid of anybody." "Why, what should we be afraid of?" asked the Horse and Donkey together, each feeling that, of course, there must be something that was going to disturb their peace of mind and the quietness of the day. "Billy the Goat," said the Magpie. "He thinks you haven't been treating him with enough respect, and he's coming here now to buck the lives out of both of you." Then the Magpie flew away. Kate Ann shivered and William shook at what the Magpie had told them, for they were a pair that were very easily affrighted.

In hops and jumps, shaking his beard and tossing his horns, Billy was coming towards them. He was as angry as any animal they had ever seen; the nearer he came the more frightened they grew of him. He was shouting out:

The crown of the causeway on roadway and street,
And the Teagues under my feet.

There was a bench near where William and Kate Ann were standing, and on this bench there were a couple of straw beehives. Billy, just to show them how strongly he was feeling, struck the bench with his horns. The hives were shaken and bees flew out. They lighted on poor Kate Ann. They stung more sorely than any goad that was ever stuck into her hide. She threw up her heels and dashed away. She galloped down the avenue and out of the gate. Then she made her way down the hillside, never to come back to the house in which there was such good provision of carrots.

William had turned aside and Billy had drawn back, and no bees had come on either of them. William shook his head as if to say, "What can it all be about?" But Billy tossed his horns and beard as if to say to him, "You'll get twice as much if you aren't careful." Then he turned and marched back to the cabbage-garden.

It was all very upsetting, William thought sadly. He

couldn't think of anything to do; he never had had much to do with goats and didn't know why they got into tempers or how they could be got out of them. Billy was very cantankerous—that was very evident now—although he had seemed such a friendly and helpful kind of goat. Perhaps in a while he would get over his cantankerousness. Waiting and thinking, his head drooping, he stood there. In a while he went into the hall and rang the bell that was on the table. He hoped to see Billy marching towards him with that alacrity that was one of the nice things about him. But no goat came out of the cabbage-garden. William sighed and shook, his head and went for a stroll alone. And now he knew that he was quite down in the dumps. If Kate Ann had been with him he would have told her the names of the rivers of Ireland; he had told her he would do that so as to improve her mind. Now there was nobody he could say a word to. He began to say over to himself the names of the rivers, but instead of the ten of yesterday he could only think of six today.

He turned back and stood before the house waiting for Billy to make some sign to him. But the goat marched past without saying one word, good or bad, to him. Yes, there was something about goats, William thought, that made one not sure of them; one couldn't really keep on terms with goats, and perhaps they were all a little crazy. He went into the stable and settled himself in the stall he had taken. Billy came in and slammed the door after him. The crickets were chirruping around as if everything was fair and quiet, and William took his few snatches of sleep; every time he wakened he heard Billy muttering in his beard and singing his party songs.

When morning broke he went, leaving Billy behind in the stable. William passed him the time of day, of course, but Billy barely answered him. He only felt like having a mouthful of hay that morning. As he was taking that mouthful the Magpie came beside him, perching on the gate-post. "You'd better be going," said she. "Going where?" said William, his knees knocking together, for he felt quite shaken. "Going back to where you came from," said the Magpie. "Mind, I warned you." Just then a hunt came over the hill and there was the baying of hounds. "They're coming," said the Magpie. "He sent for them, and they'll devour you, hoofs and hide." The bay of the hounds was very frightening to a Circus-horse that had never been in a hunt. William turned from the hayrick and went hurrying down the avenue, foam coming on his mouth from the fright he was in. Then the Magpie flew over and lighted on the door as the goat was coming out of the stable. "You'd better go while you can get away," said she to him, "the Horse is hurrying away to bring up the men who will put you in the lock-up." He snorted at her and marched into the cabbage-garden. "I'll go when

I'm made, as the Grand Master said," muttered Billy to himself.

No story's true until its end is told, and though I have come near it I'm not at the end of this story yet. Well, which of the three do you want to hear about this minute? The Donkey, is it? Kate Ann was born to be an ass to an Apple-woman and an ass to an Apple-woman she remained. As she went upon the road she met the old body coming to look for her, a halter in her hand, and she went up and put her head in the halter and was led back and put between the shafts of the cart; it was piled with apples that someone had given the old woman. She drew the cart to the market. All day she stood by the cart while one boy and another boy spent his ha'penny upon apples. She stood as she used to stand there with her head hanging down. But now Kate Ann had a many things to think about—how good carrots were and what a lot of them were in the world, and how knowledgeable William the Circus-horse was, and how near she herself had come to knowing the names of the rivers of Ireland. Thoughts were in Kate Ann's mind that day and the rest of the days that she stood in the street beside the old woman's apple-cart.

Billy was born to go with drums and be in processions, and with drums and in processions he was for the rest of his days. When the master came back to the manor and found a goat in the garden browsing on his broccoli he was as mad as a master might be, and he swore he would mulct the marauder who, as he thought, had harried his hay and colloped his carrots. He went to lay Billy by the heels. But "No Surrender," said Billy, and marched right against him. As he did the master of the house saw the flitters of ribbons on his horns and knew Billy to be as loyal and independent as he was himself. So all he did to him was to take him back to the Lodge. Billy stayed for the rest of his days and often had the chance of saying:

> *I am an Independent Man*
> *From Portadown upon the Bann,*

and

> *The crown of the causeway on roadway and street,*
> *And the Teagues under my feet.*

And William the old Circus-horse went on the road that led down from the hills. No other creature was on it, and as he stopped now and again to drink from the stream that went by he felt very lonesome. William was not one that had ever galloped much in his life, but now he remembered the times he had, and was doleful because those galloping days were over. After every drink he took he sighed deeply. What would he do with himself, he wondered. He might go into one of the wild fields here. But he felt that the nights would be very cold and that he would get stiff in all his joints if he stayed up here. He would have to go where people were. And as soon as he did someone would put a rope around his neck and lead him somewhere that it would give him a sinking feeling to go towards.

He came upon a level road. He should have known it if it had not been that the last time he was on it he was too fearful to notice the way he was going. For this was the road he had come on when Bob Cinnamon the Clown led him from the tail-end of the cart that went so fast. He was beside the Big Tree before he knew where he was. Then he remembered the place where he had spread out his feet, bringing the man down off the cart. He was back where he had been left without a master.

He stood there with his feet spread out as if he felt the rope pulling at him, with his stump of tail unlifted and his mane straggling in strings down his neck, with his knees bending and his neck drooping, and all the spirit he had had gone out of him. He didn't know whether to turn back or go on. And then there was a man beside him who put his arms around his neck. "William, my steed, you are back to me, and we'll not part from each other again."

And that was how William and Bob Cinnamon the Clown became companions once more. Bob had bought a shop in the village and was selling horse-medicines and cow-medicines and grass-seeds and whitewash-brushes. He had a stable for a horse and a three-acre field at the back of the house, and he led the old Circus-horse into one or the other of them. The place suited William very well, and in a while he got back all his spirits; he could always say to himself as many as ten, and once he got up to twelve names of the rivers of Ireland. Often Cinnamon would have him walk round the Big Tree on his hind-legs and put his fore-legs down on his master's shoulders, and this was a great delight to the children who had never been to a Circus.

WHEN I HELPED
TO MAKE A HAY-ROPE

* * *

IT was as long as a year after that before I heard another story told under the Big Tree of Bunlahy. I had gone into the village to leave back a smoothing-iron that my mother had had the loan of. I had borrowed it for her from the woman who sold pins and candies in the shop at the end of the street. (She must have sold other goods, too, but these were the only things I bought from her, though indeed I used to borrow many another thing.) Well, I had left the smoothing-iron back after giving all the thanks that my mother had told me to give, and I had turned towards home when I saw a man with a calf beside the Big Tree. The calf was young and didn't want to go to a strange place, and the man wanted to make a hay-rope to lead her along. But it takes two to make a hay-rope, or a suguan as we used to call it, and until I appeared there was nobody but the man himself to be seen. So he beckoned me to come over to him.

THE "MOUNTAINY" MAN

To make a suguan one takes a wisp of hay and puts a twist in it and adds wisp to wisp, lengthening it out while the other holds the bit made, walking backwards as wisp after wisp is twisted into it. He had a heap of hay beside him, and he had me hold the twist he made while he added to it, I walking backwards from the tree as the rope lengthened. I never saw the man before and I was never to see him afterwards: he was dressed in an old-fashioned way, with knee-breeches and a half-top hat, so I think he was from the mountains. And as we went on lengthening the rope, he standing under the Big Tree, he told this story to me. He didn't put a name on it, but I'll name it now:

THE TWO YOUTHS WHOSE FATHER
WAS UNDER THE SEA

ONCE upon a time, and if it wasn't upon my time nor upon your time, it was upon a good time, anyway, when jackdaws built their nests in old men's beards, and turkeys went up and down the laneways smoking pipes of tobacco, and the roofs of the houses of Bunlahy were thatched with pancakes, and ponies, saddled and all, went along the roadways, saying, "Who's for a ride, who's for a ride?" Well, in those times there were two brothers whose names were Jack Sea and John Sea, and they were named Jack and John because there was no difference between them—one had the same appearance as the other.

One day one of them was swimming with other boys and he swam farther than any of them. Then the other brother who was standing with the lookers-on heard a boy say, "So far can Jack Sea swim, and yet he doesn't know who his father is, or where he lives, or if he lives at all." When John Sea heard this said he made up his mind that he would not rest until he knew who his father was, and where he lived, or if he lived at all. So he went back to the house and told his grandfather what was in his mind to do. His grandfather filled a basket with provisions for him and told him he had his leave to go seek his father. "But whether you should go east or west, or north or south, I don't know, for your father was never seen was no longer on our land." If his mother had been there (but she alive) she would have told him that her father had sent her to fish on a certain day, telling her to land only what came heavy upon her line. She had gone out on the sea in a boat; she had felt a very heavy pull, and she had let the boat drift until she had come to an island. There she had landed what was on her line, and, behold! it was a young man and a very princely-looking young man. She and he had lived on the island as man and wife until a night came when he had said, "I am drawn back to the sea by the power of the Hag of the Waves. Beware of her sister, the Hag of the Hollows." The Fisherman's daughter never saw him again. He went under the waves, and she took her boat and went back to her father's. A while afterwards she had children, twins, and they were Jack Sea and John Sea.

So John Sea started out with his basket of provisions, and before he left the house his grandfather said to him, "Leave the knife that was your father's, and if the blade gets rusty we'll know that something has befallen you and your brother will go in search of you." He went straight on from the door of his grandfather's house. He had been going from the full of daylight to the fall of dark when he sat down under a big tree and began to eat provisions out of his basket. As he did a red Fox came across the hill, and stepping to where he sat looked at him as if he wanted something from him. So John Sea took provision out of his basket, and gave it to him, and the red Fox ate standing beside him. Then the Fox said, "The hungry season is upon us, John Sea, and if you give me provision for my wife and my young ones, I'll not forget it to you." John Sea put his hand into the basket and gave him bread and meat and plenty of it. "My thanks to you, John Sea, and if ever you are in danger, call on the red Fox of the Three Rocks and he'll come to your help." And saying this the red Fox went across the hill.

Where he was when the sun sank, there he rested, and the next day he went on again. And so he was resting and traveling and traveling and resting until he came to a Giant's castle that was between a deep wood and a wide sea. There he asked for work and work was given him. It was to tend the pigs. He took out the drove to the wood in the morning, and in the evening he brought them back to the cave where their lairs were. And for his first month's work he was given a hawk, and for his second month's work he was given a hound, and for his third month's work he was given a horse. So John Sea fared, and in that time not a speck of rust came on the blade of the knife that hung against the wall of his grandfather's house.

One night when he was lying in the moonlight outside the cave where the Giant's pigs were grunting and turning and turning and grunting, he heard a purring, and when he looked up he saw a running hare. She ran round him once, and ran round him twice, and ran round him for the third time, and as she did the hare said:

John Sea, John Sea,
Follow you me;
Follow me, John,
And your quest is won.

John Sea rose from where he was resting, mounted his horse, took his hawk upon his shoulder, and rode where the hare ran.

She ran into the deep of the wood, and John Sea on his horse, with his hawk and his hound, followed her. But when he was under the oak branches of the midwood he lost sight of the hare. He stopped there and he made a shelter of branches and moss; he placed himself within it, with his horse and his hawk and his hound; they were closed from the creatures of the night and the dark wood.

His hound had taken a bird from the ground and his hawk had taken a bird from the air, and John Sea struck fire to cook the birds for his supper. As the light of the fire went through the branches of the shelter, he heard purring again, and then he heard a hand upon the door, and then a crying voice saying, "Let me to your fire and your shelter! Let me in, let me in!"

"Who are you that are out with the things of the night and the things of the dark wood?"

"An old woman I am, weary, weary."

"Not of good kind can you be who are with the things of the night and the things of the dark wood."

"I am an old woman, and if you won't let me to your fire and your shelter, I die, I die."

"Old woman, I will let you in."

"But your horse, your hound, and your hawk will attack me, I know."

"What shall I do, then, with my horse, my hound, and my hawk?"

"Tether them, tether them, tether them with this. When they are tethered I'll come into your shelter."

She handed him a hair of her head, a long hair. With that hair he tied his hawk, his hound, and his horse. Then he opened the door. She came to the fire, a bent old woman with a pointed chin, and a beak of a nose, and a brown, rusty cloak upon her. "Where are you, hawk?" she said. "Oh, I'm tied tightly, tightly, tied by my master." "Where are you, hound?" she said. "Oh, I'm tied tightly, tightly, tied by my master." "Where are you, horse?" she said. "Oh, I'm tied tightly, tightly, tied by my master." She took up the birds and pulled them to pieces and ate them, feathers and all. "And since the horse, the hound, and the hawk are tethered I can do what I came to do," she said. "I am the hare that led you far, John Sea, and I am the Hag of the Hollows, and this is where the quest for your father ends." She took a rod that was under her rusty cloak and struck him with it, and John Sea fell on the ground, changed into a stone that was blue like the sea. She went her way then, and when daylight came the horse, the hound, and the hawk broke the tether that held them and went back to the Giant's castle.

The blade that was hanging against the wall in the Fisherman's house became rusty all over, and Jack Sea went to search for his brother, his grandfather filling a basket with provisions for him. From the door of his grandfather's house he went straight on. He had been going from the full of daylight to the fall of dark when he sat down under a big tree and began to eat provisions out of his basket. And as he did an Eagle flew down and crouched before him. Jack Sea took provision out of the basket and gave it to the Eagle, and the Eagle ate it heartily. Then she said, "The hungry season is upon us, Jack Sea, and if you give me provision for my young ones, I'll not forget you." Jack Sea put his hand into the basket and gave her bread and meat and plenty of it, and the Eagle, taking it in her claws and rising up, said, "My thanks to you, Jack Sea, and if ever you are in danger, call on the

Eagle of the One Rock, and she'll come to your help." And saying this the Eagle flew away.

Where the sun sank, there he rested, and the next day he went on again. And he was resting and traveling, traveling and resting, till he came to the Giant's castle that was between the deep wood and the wide sea. There he asked for work and work was given him. It was to tend the Giant's cattle. He took out the herd to the pasture in the morning, and in the evening he brought them back to the cave where their byre was. And for the first month's work he was given a hawk, and for the second month's work he was given a hound, and for the third month's work he was given a horse. But no one knew how he fared, for the knife that had been hanging against the wall of the Fisherman's house he had brought with him.

One night when he was lying in the moonlight outside the cave where the Giant's cattle were lowing and bellowing, he heard a purring, and when he looked up he saw a running hare. She ran round him once, and she ran round him twice, and she ran round him for the third time, and as she did the hare said:

> *John Sea, John Sea,*
> *Follow you me;*
> *Follow me, John,*
> *And your quest end this night.*

Jack Sea rose from where he was resting, mounted his horse, took his hawk upon his shoulder, and rode where the hare ran.

He followed her into the deep of the wood. Under the oak branches of the mid-wood he lost sight of her. He stopped there and he made a shelter of branches and moss; he placed himself within it with his horse, his hawk, and his hound.

His hound had taken a bird from the ground and his hawk had taken a bird from the air, and Jack Sea struck fire to cook the birds for his supper. He heard the purring again. He heard a hand upon the door. He heard a crying voice saying, "Let me to your fire and your shelter! Let me in, let me in!"

"Who are you that are out with the things of the night and the things of the dark wood?"

"An old woman I am, weary, weary."

"Not of good kind can you be to be out with the things of the night and the things of the dark wood."

"I am an old woman, and if you don't let me in to your fire and your shelter, I die, I die."

"Old woman, I will let you in."

"But your horse, your hound, and your hawk will attack me, I know."

"What shall I do, then, with my horse, my hound, and my hawk?"

"Tether them, tether them, tether them with this. When they are tethered I'll come into your shelter."

She handed him a long hair, a hair of her head. He threw the hair into the fire. There was a crackling then.

"What is that that is crackling? How can I come in until I know what is crackling?"

"The pitch that is in the wood is crackling, for a fire is burning. And now I open the door for you, and that's all I'll do."

So she came in with her brown, rusty cloak about her. "Where are you, hawk?" she said. "Where are you, hound? Where are you, horse?" And when hawk and hound and horse answered her she took up the birds that were on the ground and pulled them to pieces and ate them, feathers and all. "I am the hare that led you so far, and I am the Hag of the Hollows, and this is where your quest ends, Jack Sea," she said. As she did the hawk flew at her, the hound sprang at her, the horse struck her with a hoof. Down she went upon the ground, and she had Jack Sea standing above her, his father's knife in his hand. And when she saw the blade she said, "Do not use it on me and I'll bring your brother back to you." "What else will you do for me if I spare you, Hag of the Hollows?" "I will show you how to come to your father." "Your life is spared you.

At her bidding he struck with her rod the blue stone

that was in the wood, and his brother, John Sea, stood
before him. She told them how they might come to their
father. "The Hag of the Waves keeps him in the caves of
the sea. Until she is dead and gone he cannot come up
from where he is. Her life depends upon an Egg. That
Egg is in a Duck, and that Duck is in the Stag that is on
the Brow of the Bare Mountain. When you get the Egg
go to the High Cliff and break it with the blade of the
knife you have. The Hag of the Waves will be no more
after that is done, and then you will see your father."
They let the Hag of the Hollows go from them and Jack
Sea and John Sea went back to the Giant's castle.

They spent their days searching for the Stag of the
Bare Mountain. Once, when they were not ready for
hunting him, the Stag came down from the top of the
Mountain. Bending his head that had big antlers upon it
he ran at them. All the weapons they had was the knife
that Jack Sea carried. "Fox of the Three Rocks, help us,
for we're in danger," John Sea cried out. Then, as the Stag
ran at them, the Fox crossed him, and going between his
legs, threw him down. On the ground lay the Stag of the
Bare Mountain. Jack Sea struck between his antlers, and
where the knife pierced a blue Duck flew up. She would
have got away only Jack Sea cried out, "Eagle of the One
Rock, we're in danger; come and help us." Then the Eagle
appeared in the sky and circled round the Duck. Down

came the Duck; she settled on the ground, and under the wings of the Eagle she laid the Egg. "Thanks to you, Fox of the Three Rocks; thanks to you, Eagle of the One Rock," the brothers cried as they took up the Egg. They went then to the High Cliff that looked over the sea.

And there, running up and down like the bird that is called the Gobadaun, was a figure like the Hag of the Hollows. She cried out to them when she saw Jack Sea and John Sea on the cliff above her. One held the Egg in his hand, the other struck it with the blade of his knife. As the Egg broke the figure below turned to foam, the brown foam on the waves that in a while was blown away.

Then the brothers saw a man rise up from the sea, and they both ran down to where he stood. And he, seeing the knife in the hands of one of the brothers, put his arms around both. Princely-looking was he. But when Jack Sea and John Sea looked upon him, they knew that he was not one whom they could ever walk with, not one they could ever speak about. They stood silent as he was silent; in a while he went from them and back into the sea, putting into his belt the knife that Jack Sea held to him.

But if he took the knife he gave them other things; on the arm of each he put a great ring of gold. And when they went back to where their grandfather lived, the young men there looked at the arm-rings and said, "John Sea and Jack Sea know who their father is, and we know that he is no common man." But the brothers did not stay to hear what was said about them. Bidding their grandfather a kind farewell, they went back to the Giant's castle. I believe they married the Giant's two daughters, and came to own castle and pasture and wood.

> *So stretch the rope*
> *With twists of hay,*
> *And if they didn't live happy,*
> *That we may!*

ON BONE-FIRE NIGHT

* * *

I remember a Bone-fire Night when the street here was as lively as any street you were ever on. We made the Bone-fire in the middle of it, a little way down from the Big Tree, and when it blazed up we could see the faces of the old people who were seated there, and the old wall of Baron's Hall, and the high trees that grew inside, and the frog that went hopping from one side of the street to the other. People came up the Bog Road and down the Mountain Road to be at the Bone-fire in Bunlahy. For this isn't like other parts of the parish—a place where there isn't a tree nor a bush; we have plenty to burn hereabouts, and the boys spent the latter part of Midsummer's Eve (or St. John's Eve if you like to call it that) pulling up stumps of old trees and pulling down old bushes and digging up old tree-trunks in the bog and carrying all the wood down to the Big Tree. There are whin-bushes on the hillside, too; they only make a blaze,

but they make a good blaze, and we cut them with bill-
hooks and had them ready to start the fire and to throw
upon it when we wanted a blaze. I was out most of the
day helping to carry the wood, and when the boys lighted
the fire I was as proud as if I had a queen for an aunt. We
had a piper to play for us, and we had dancing, and we
had the boys throwing a heavy stone across the road, one
throwing farther than the other, and we had songs and
good ones from the Shoemaker's daughter, Grace. It was
a real Bone-fire Night, with sport and high spirits lasting
through all the hours that the blaze went up. Well, as the
saying is:

> *Time can wear down every stone;*
> *Ireland's eagles all have flown!*

and no Bone-fire is lighted beside the Big Tree any more.
While the boys were dancing, or throwing the stone, or
whispering to the girls, the old men were telling about
old happenings, and in a while they were asking Martin
the Weaver to tell them a tale that only he had aright. I
came from where I was casting logs upon the blaze and
stayed beside the old man while the story was being told.
They were all seated fornenst the Bone-fire, and the blaze
was upon Martin's face and hands, and upon the staff he
raised up when he wanted particular attention paid to the

part he was telling at the time. The story he told on that Midsummer's-Eve Night I will name:

THE WIZARD EARL

TO gather Fern-seed and get any good out of it, you must gather it on Midsummer's Eve just as the sun is going down, neither a minute before nor a minute after. The Fern-seed gathered at such time lets you walk unseen by mortal eyes; you can be here and you can be there and no one will either see or know you. But you have to be very watchful when you are about to gather the seed; beings are abroad that will try to do you harm, and will be able to do it if all your wits and all your mind aren't on your purpose. For that reason you mustn't have people watching while you're doing it—they will scatter your wits if you know that they are there.

Gerald, the Earl of Kildare, who lived in the great castle of Maynooth, got ready to gather Fern-seed on a certain Midsummer's Eve. Besides being the Earl of Kildare he was a Wizard, and the people who had seen him making spells and working wonders called him the Wizard Earl. Why such a great Wizard as he was had waited so long to gather the seed that would let him go unseen I don't know; perhaps he had had harder things to do and things that had to be done first. Be that as it may, at a time in his life when he was well advanced in wizardry, Earl Gerald went up a hillside to be ready to gather the Fern-seed at the right minute of Midsummer's Eve. He had all his wits and all his mind in harness, and he was ready to say the spell:

Let me unseen
Go and stand,
Fern-seed
On my left hand!

when he saw heads watching him from behind every stone on the hillside. The country people had expected his coming and were there to watch all he did. He was very angry, and if he had had a sword in his belt he would have cut many of the heads off. But you may not carry iron with you when you are out on Midsummer's Eve and amongst enchantments. Earl Gerald carried no sword. He changed himself into a Stag with high and wide antlers and stood there threatening the people who had come to watch him. They went helter-skelter away. But it was too late then for the Wizard Earl to gather the Fern-seed that would let him walk and stand unseen.

He changed back into his own proper form and went down the hillside and into his Castle. He went into a secret chamber where he used to read by the light of a magic lamp; it was the light of this lamp streaming

HE CHANGED HIMSELF TO A STAG AND STOOD THERE
THREATENING THE PEOPLE.

brightly through the slit in the wall that had made the
servants and the country people around take notice of his
wizardries. He stood reading a deep book of magic that
was propped up before his eyes when a knocking came
upon the door of the chamber. He opened the door and
there stood his young Countess.

"I wanted to see what your secret chamber is like,
Gerald," said she.

"Yes, my love," he said, "but I was going up on the
Tower to look at the stars in tonight's sky."

"Won't you take me up with you, Gerald," said she, "and tell me the names of the stars?"

"I will," said the Wizard Earl, quenching the magic lamp and leaving the chamber in darkness which was what he wanted to do, for there were things in the chamber that he did not want her to look upon.

They went up the winding stair and out on the top of the Tower. Behind them went Cogan, the Monkey that belonged to the Castle. People thought that the Monkey was there to help the Earl in his wizardries. But that wasn't so; a Monkey was kept in Maynooth Castle for the reason that a Monkey had saved the life of an infant heir: the place had taken fire, the child was in a burning room, and a Monkey that had been made a pet of had taken him up, and, holding him with one arm, had scrambled to the branch of a tree and had held the infant heir until his master and mistress called to him to come down. Ever since that had happened a Monkey was kept in Maynooth Castle; there is a Monkey on the Fitzgerald plate to this day.

Well, the Earl and Countess with Cogan behind them went to the top of the Tower. Earl Gerald and his lady saw Bone-fires burning on every side; there were shoutings and lowings, for the country people were driving their cattle through the fires as they used to until some years ago; they did this to free them from any evil power that might be upon them. From the fires they looked to the sky; it was clear and lovely. He began to tell her about the stars, and his arm went about her as they stood by the parapet looking up at the sky. The Countess wasn't more than a girl, and as Earl Gerald spoke to her he remembered that he hadn't given her much of his company since they were wedded, for his wizardries had taken up his days and his nights. But he would forget them for a while, he thought, and get to know his beautiful Countess.

"But I will never get to know you, Gerald," said she, as he clasped her hand.

"Why do you say that, my Duck of Diamonds?" said he.

"Because you can change yourself into so many shapes. As soon as I knew you in one you would change into another shape."

"How do you know I can change shapes?" asked the Wizard Earl.

"The country people saw you do it. I have heard all about it from the maids. You frightened the people terribly, you wicked shape-changer."

"I should have frightened them more. I should have left them speechless."

"But how will I ever get to know you in all your shapes?" said the lady.

"You need know me only in one, my Cluster of Nuts," said he.

"I should never know you at all if I only knew you in one, you shape-shifter," said she.

"Well, the truth is," said he, "that there are only a few shapes I can change into. The country people think I can change into a thousand, but that isn't so. Three is the most I can manage."

"Let me see them—oh, let me see them," said the Countess, taking his face between her hands.

"Don't ask for that—you mustn't ask for that," said he.

"Oh, but why not?" said she. "Let me see your three shapes—let me see them now and I'll never ask to see them again."

"It cannot be," said he.

"Not even if your Countess asked you lovingly on a night like this?" said she.

"My White Calf," said the Earl, "if I changed shapes, and if anyone who loved me was made afraid by the change—Now, are you listening to this?"

"I am, my love."

"If anyone who loved me was made afraid by the change, I'd have to disappear. No mortal would ever see me again."

"Is that true?" she asked.

"It is true," he told her very solemnly.

"Where would you disappear to?"

"I'd have to go into the Fairy Mounds. I'd live a long time there—hundreds of years—but mortals would never see me again except on Midsummer Eves. And you might be frightened by the change I made."

"I'd never be made afraid. I'd know it was you who were there, you old Wizard."

"I'm afraid, and very much afraid, that you'd be afraid," he said.

"I couldn't be made afraid," said she. "How could I? I'd know it was you. And I'd be made miserable every day to think that you could change into shapes I had never seen. The country people have seen you as some wonderful thing, but I never have. Now wouldn't you change your shape for the sake of the neglected wife you brought into your big Castle and have never done anything to pleasure?"

"Will you not be afraid?"

"No."

"And you'll remember that it is I?"

"Of course I will. And I'll love you so much when I've seen you do these wonderful things. Give me a kiss now and nothing will frighten me."

So he kissed her and she kissed him back, and he turned away and muttered the spell that changed his shape. Then the Countess saw a great Stag with lowered antlers standing before her. Her breath came quickly, and then she said, "I'm not afraid." The Stag moved away, and in a while Earl Gerald stood before her.

"I wasn't a bit afraid," said she. "Now go and change into something else, my Share of the World."

He did. He changed into a Cat-of-the-Mountain that stood staring at her with unwinking eyes. "I'm not afraid," said she, but she was—just a little bit. The Cat drew back from her, and then, as before, Earl Gerald showed himself. "And now for this change," he said, "and then you'll have seen me in all the shapes I can change into. I'm not afraid that you'll be made frightened by this."

He changed before her eyes. He remained the same Earl Gerald, but Earl Gerald become so tiny that he wasn't up to her knee. And she was so enchanted by this shape that she cried out to him not to change back for a while. She watched him as he walked across the floor that was the top of the Tower, going over to the parapet, as small and as fine a figure as ever walked, she said to herself. She loved the Earl doubly, she thought, now that he was so much like a small child.

And then she screamed out, for the Monkey that had been squatting in the shadows made a bound and lifted the little one up in his long arms. And hearing her scream, he sprang up on the parapet. "Oh, I'm frightened, I'm frightened!" cried the lady, as she saw the Monkey leaning over, the changed Earl in his arms. There was a sigh as if the night-wind passed over her, and when she went to where Cogan was there was nothing in his arms. The Monkey jumped down from the parapet and crouched in a corner. The Earl had disappeared.

Then she ran down the stairway calling to the servants, and they got lights and ran outside with her. They searched all round to see if he had fallen from the Tower, but no trace of him was to be found. He had disappeared; he had gone into the Fairy Mounds.

The young Countess grew old; she died; another Earl and another Countess lived in the great Castle of Maynooth. Other Earls and other Countesses lived and grew old there and died. Stones fell from the walls, grass grew around where the Tower stood; the Castle was demolished, and a new house for the Earls was built near by. But still Earl Gerald lived on. He lived in the Fairy Mounds with the heroes who are to help in the deliverance of the land and he was their leader.

On Midsummer Eves he rides abroad with a train of horsemen. The horses of the other riders have no shoes on their hoofs; Earl Gerald's horse has, but they are not iron; they are silver shoes. When those shoes are worn thin he will know that the time has come when the

people are ready to take help from himself and his horsemen. One Midsummer Eve a man who was crossing
the Curragh of Kildare saw a single rider going towards
where a company of riders waited for him. "Has the time
come?" they shouted. And the rider said, "Not yet, not
yet!" That was just before Earl Gerald's descendant,
Lord Edward Fitzgerald, was making the people ready
for an uprising.

And another Midsummer's Eve, not so long ago, a
very lordly-looking man rode up to a blacksmith's forge
in the long twilight. He dismounted, and the blacksmith,
coming outside to attend to the horse, lifted a hoof up,
and, behold! the shoe was of silver, and the nails that fastened it were of silver too. He raised the second, and the
third, and the fourth hoof, and the shoe on each was of
silver and fastened with silver nails. "I have no metal to
match what is here, my Lord," said the blacksmith. "I
do not want them repaired," said the lordly-looking man.
"What I want is to know how many miles' traveling they
will have to do before they are worn thin?" "Two hundred miles, my Lord," said the blacksmith. "It will not
take many more Midsummer's Eves," said the man, as he
mounted the silver-shod horse and rode away. That was
Earl Gerald as sure as we are standing by this Bone-fire.
And some of us will live to see the Midsummer Eve when
he and his riders will come out on the Curragh of Kildare,

he with his horse's silver shoes worn as thin as they can
be worn.

WHEN WE FOUND
THE TREASURE

* * *

AFTER that Midsummer's Night I happened to be helping Martin the Weaver. It wasn't at his loom, though,
but in the bog where he owned a piece of ground. For
the help I gave I was to get a few panniers of peat; we
needed them in my mother's house, for we had very little
to make our fire with. I remember to this day the sight of
my mother's donkey with the panniers slung across her,
a gray little beast in the black of the bog, and myself in
my bare feet carrying the sods of peat over to where she
stood. But my job was to help Martin to drag up some
pieces of bog-deal that were under the peat—old trunks
of trees that had belonged, perhaps, to a forest that was
there a thousand years ago. Well, as I was standing in a
bog-hole and trying to raise a big piece of timber that was
there, I sank down through the soft peat. Then I noticed
another piece of timber by the edge of the black pit. I
dragged it out and found that it was shaped like a black

box. I lifted it up and brought it to Martin. "It's a chest," Martin said, and then he pulled the lid up or the sides out of it, and, lo and behold! there was gold in it and beads that were the size and the color of chestnuts. "By the Rock of Cashel," said Martin, "it's a King's treasure you have come on!" Well, we hurried to his house, he carrying the chest and I driving my mother's donkey with its panniers filled with peat. A King's treasure and firing for the hearth, I kept saying to myself, thinking how strange it was that peat and the rich ornaments should have come out of the same bog.

Well, we took out the beads and a golden collar and left them on Martin's loom and tried to understand what our find amounted to. I don't know how it came about, but an hour hadn't gone by before half the parish was in to look at what we had found in the bog. And then Father Maurice came to the door and asked leave to look at the treasure. It was he who told us what we should do. These things did not belong to the finders, it seemed, but to the government of the country; he wrote a letter to the people who should be written to about treasures found—to the people in the Museum—and he told Martin to keep the find safe until someone in authority came down to look it over.

And in a few days a man from the Museum came to Martin's house—a great scholar he was, and he told us

FATHER MAURICE

that the beads were as precious as the gold; they were big pieces of amber that went to make the necklace of the Queen whose partner wore the collar that was with them—a deep collar of pure gold. These were ornaments that had been worn and hidden away two thousand years ago, he said, perhaps after some battle. And he thought that where they had been there was likelihood of other treasures being found, too. So he took me with him to help him to search around the place where I had come upon the chest. And he found other things there—sword-blades and another chest that was filled with small golden rings—the rings that were the money of two thousand years ago. Martin was rewarded for keeping the treasure safe. And I was well rewarded for finding it and for helping the scholar to find the other things. I was put through school and college by the authorities of the Museum, and put in the way of becoming, myself, something of a scholar in the old things of the country.

This scholar who came amongst us was as friendly as any neighbor could be. He liked nothing better than long discussions with Kevin the Shoemaker, and Martin the Weaver, and old Patch the Nailer. Indeed, I heard him say that he would have to go far to find men as knowledgeable as these men were. He would sit under the Big Tree with them and listen for the whole of an evening to what they had to tell about the things of the countryside—things that only they remembered. He told them stories of the old times—stories that had been written down a thousand years ago. I remember one evening when the sword-blades we had found were lying on the ground before the seat, or stuck in the ground around the Big Tree, hearing him tell this story:

WHEN THE LUPRACHAUNS CAME TO IRELAND

ONCE upon a time the smallest of small men came to the court of Fergus, King of Ulster. Eisirt was his name. So manful was the mannikin, and so full of witty discourse and melodious poetry, that the King wanted to keep him always at the court. But Eisirt appealed to the King's men of lore and learning, and they, seeing that he bore the wand that showed that he was a man of lore and learning amongst his own people, would not permit Fergus to hold him against his will. He was given permission to leave Ulster, and Ae, the King's dwarf, was let go with him to visit amongst the Luchra and the Luchrapaun, as Eisirt named his people.

Eisirt with Ae who looked like a giant beside him set out on a journey to the sea-shore. As they went on, Ae would get far ahead, his legs being longer than his companion's. Eisirt had to do much running to keep up with the King's dwarf. At nightfall they reached the sea-shore, and they wrapped themselves in their cloaks and lay down to sleep until daybreak. When dawn came, Ae, finding out that no boat was waiting for them, despaired of getting across the sea. "My King's fairy steed will come for us," said Eisirt, "and mounted on that steed we can cross the waves." Even as this was said Ae saw something moving over the water to them. It seemed a bird skimming the waves at first. Then it looked like a hare running across a plain. It came upon the shore; it was a little horse of yellow color with eyes keen and bright as a hawk's. "You can ride upon this steed, but I cannot ride upon it," said Ae, "and the pair of us certainly could not have room on its back." "Mount behind me, Ae," said Eisirt, "and be not afraid that your load of learning will break the back of King Iubdaun's fairy steed." So King Fergus's dwarf, placing himself behind his companion, mounted the steed and the pair were carried across the waves and to the land of the Luchra and the Luchrapaun.

As they rode on together, Eisirt told Ae the reason why he had gone to Ireland and why he was bringing him back with him. It was because of the King of the Luchra and the Luchrapaun. Iubdaun was a very proud monarch. He was proud not only because he ruled over two such mighty peoples, not only because he had an army of seven battalions of brawny warriors, not only because his champion, Glomar, the son of Glos, could hew down a thistle with a single stroke of his sword and overthrow twelve men in a wrestling-bout, but he was proud of his own self, and he was particularly proud of his own good looks. His people had all fair hair, but the King's was as black as jet and fell curling to his shoulders; his skin was as white as the foam of the wave, and his cheeks were as red as

"YOU CAN RIDE UPON THIS STEED," SAID AE TO KING
FERGUS'S DWARF.

rowan berries. Everyone spoke of his beauty, and it was
in his beauty that Iubdaun's pride was fixed.

He had possessions that added to his pride. He owned
a spear that could kill a hundred men in battle, a shield
which no weapon could ever strike through, a girdle of
silver that kept the one who wore it from sickness. Two
new treasures had been added to these: a pair of shoes
that could carry the wearer over the water, or under the
water, or on the bed of the water; a wand which drew

the love of every lady in the land to the one who held it. These new treasures had made Iubdaun more proud even than he had been before. And Eisirt believed that the lady who had loved him had given her love to the King when he had come, the wand in his hand, to where she was.

The King's pride and Eisirt's temper had been shown at a banquet which Iubdaun had given to the nobles of the Luchra and the Luchrapaun. When the cup-bearers had served the heady liquors and when the company were beginning to talk loudly, the King had arisen, and, holding his many-colored drinking-horn in his hand, had said to those present there, "Have ye ever beheld a better King than I am?" And the nobles of the Luchra and the Luchrapaun had answered with one voice, "We have never beheld a better King."

"And have ye or any others ever beheld a better champion than my champion, Glomar, the son of Glos?" "Neither we nor any others have ever laid eyes on a better champion," they had answered.

"Or any warriors mightier than the seven battalions that guard this, my royal dwelling, under the command of Beg, the son of Beg?" "Neither we nor any others ever beheld such mighty warriors, on our words," they had answered him.

"I cannot be wrong, then, when I declare that none

of the world's armies is fit to carry off captives or treasures from the house we are banqueting in, my royal house, guarded as it is by such a mighty army, and having within it such a powerful champion and such mighty princes, not to speak of myself, the King," Iubdaun had said proudly. And the nobles of the Luchra and the Luchrapaun had shouted out that none of the world's armies would venture near where they were.

Now Eisirt being a man of lore and learning knew that in lands beyond the sea there were greater powers than Iubdaun or the princes and nobles had ever dreamt of; the King's pride and boastfulness had made him angry, and he was out of temper because the lady who had once loved him was watching Iubdaun with rapture; he had laughed, and all who heard it knew there was mockery in his laugh.

"Why do you laugh, Eisirt?" said the King, turning to him.

"I laugh because I know that the warriors of a single province of Ireland could take your seven battalions, the house, and the treasures that are in it, and the champion and all the princes and nobles present, without suffering the loss of a single man, O King," said Eisirt.

"Seize ye this man of lore and learning," the King had commanded, and the guards had laid their hands upon him. "Thou hast done ill, O King, to have this done to me," Eisirt had cried, "I have only said what all men of lore and learning know to be true." And then he had said in the hearing of all, "The King owes it to our learned order that I be given three days to prove the truth of what I have declared," and those who were present had said, "It is just that the King give Eisirt this respite."

So King Iubdaun had to give Eisirt three days' respite, and he had also to allow him the use of his fairy steed for the crossing to Ireland and the crossing back again, Eisirt giving pledges that he would return within three days and accept the King's judgment. Then, mounted on the fairy steed, he had gone over to Ireland, and to King Fergus's royal dwelling in Emain Macha in Ulster, and what had befallen him there need not be told you.

The seven battalions of the royal army were drawn up on the shore to await Eisirt's coming. When he dismounted and they saw Ae dismounting they cried out, "Eisirt has brought a giant with him to destroy us all." The seven battalions would have fled if Beg and Glomar and King Iubdaun himself had not forced them to stand their ground. Then, even although the one with him looked so big and so fierce, Iubdaun walked royally over to Eisirt, greeted him, and welcomed his man of lore and learning back from the country of the Big Men.

All knew that Eisirt had the right to inflict a penalty on the King who had accused him of giving false testimony and had had him seized by his guards. All waited anxiously to hear what penalty he would inflict on King Iubdaun. After a feast that was given him Eisirt rose up and said to those who were present, "I made a journey into Ireland and I have returned, and I declare to you that the one I have brought back with me is the least in stature of the men who are there. And now I lay a penalty upon King Iubdaun: It is that he himself go over to Ireland, enter the house that I have been in, and taste, before any of his household tastes it, the porridge that is prepared for the King of Ulster's breakfast."

On hearing this sentence the bright color went from King Iubdaun's cheeks and his heart sank down within him. For a while he had the intention of refusing to leave his realm. But when he turned to his wife, the Lady Bebo, she said, "The penalty is just and you must submit to it. This very day we shall go across to Ireland, you and I. You shall accomplish what has been laid upon you—in the morning you shall taste the porridge that has been prepared for the King of Ulster's breakfast, and without more ado we shall return to the realm of the Luchra and the Luchrapaun."

Then Iubdaun ordered his fairy steed to be brought to him. He mounted it and Bebo mounted behind him; they went over the waves and crossed the main sea, and came to the shore of Ireland. They bade the fairy steed

return to their realm and come back for them at daylight and await their coming to the shore, and then they
made their way to the King of Ulster's dwelling. They
slipped within as the porters were closing the doors and
hid behind the shoes the guards had taken off. When the
fires were raked and the candles quenched and the king's
household had gone to their sleeping-chambers, Iubdaun
and Bebo, holding each other's hands, made their way
downstairs and into the wide kitchen. They rested there,
sleeping uneasily upon a spread of rushes that was in a
corner. Then, when the first gleam of light came, they
looked around for the pot in which the King of Ulster's
porridge had been cooked.

The pots grew out of the darkness of the kitchen as
mountains grow out of a countryside when the sun rises.
These pots were tremendous. There were pots of iron
and pots of copper and pots of bronze. Over the ashes of
the great hearth there hung an iron pot that a battalion of
King Iubdaun's army could barely put their joined hands
around. This was the Cauldron of Emain Macha, and in
it was cooked the porridge for the whole of King Fergus's
household. Pot after pot was on the hearth and the hobs.
Then Iubdaun and Bebo saw a pot that they knew was
the King's pot—it had silver upon its rim. It stood upon
three legs a little way out of the ashes of the hearth. There
was no lid upon this pot.

"Mount quickly; put your hand in and scoop up some of the porridge; taste it, and then let us be off before the household stirs," said Bebo to her lord. But it was not easy for Iubdaun to mount to the opening of the pot. They pushed out chips and bits of logs that were lying by the hearth, and, working together, they built up a platform that reached to the edge of the pot. Iubdaun mounted while Bebo strove to keep the platform from falling down. Reaching the rim, he leant out to scoop up the porridge that was near the pot's top. He overbalanced and fell into it. He struggled to get his head and shoulders out; he succeeded, but he remained up to his waist in the porridge.

Bebo waited anxiously; she thought that Iubdaun could clamber back and that he was making a needless delay where he was. "Do not stay," she cried, "we must be away before daylight is at the full. The fairy steed will not wait for us if we stay long." No word of triumph came from the pot. "There are dangers all around us," Bebo cried. Then she heard the heavy voice of her lord saying, "My feet are held fast and I cannot move. But you, Bebo, hurry away. Mount the fairy steed and ride back to our realm. It is my fate to be taken captive by the Big People."

"Iubdaun, is it you who speak thus? Have you not told me often and often that nothing could hold you against your will? Loose yourself and come out of the pot at once."

"I cannot move. Leave me here; take the fairy steed and return."

"That I will not. Here I stay until I know how it will fare with you." So Iubdaun and Bebo discoursed from within and from without the pot.

There was a stirring in the King's house; there was a hurry of footsteps, a clatter of people coming down to the kitchen. There was a cloud of ashes from the hearth as the fuel was flung down. There was a blaze of fire. There was a big scullion dropping a pot as Bebo rushed out from where she crouched, and the sight of Iubdaun stuck fast in the porridge, and loud shouting, and the coming of other scullions.

They lifted Iubdaun out of the porridge; they took little Bebo up from the floor; they brought the pair to Fergus who was still in his royal bed. "He has come back and brought his wife with him," said Fergus when Iubdaun and Bebo were set beside him. "No, it is not the mannikin who was here before," he said as he looked Iubdaun over. "That one had fair hair and this one's locks are black as jet. Who are you, little man?"

"I am Iubdaun, the son of Abdaun, King of the Luchra and the Luchrapaun," said Iubdaun with the majestic air that was proper to him. "This is my queen, Bebo. We are hostages in your house, and we know that you will treat us in a our rank."

"Ho, ho," laughed King Fergus, "you have spirit, lit-tle man. I shall treat you as a boon companion."

He had Iubdaun and Bebo placed in a chamber where they were waited on by the King's children; they were not in danger of being stifled by the breath of the servitors and big guards or knocked over by their lumbering and blundering movements. In a while Bebo was permitted to leave Emain Macha and go to the place the fairy steed returned to every morning to await them. She parted from Iubdaun with many lamentations and with promises to do everything to obtain his release should King Fergus detain him, and she went back to the realm of the Luchra and the Luchrapaun.

As for Iubdaun, he gave his word that he would not attempt to escape and he was given the liberty of King Fergus's house. All the household were charmed by his looks and his wise and witty discourse. He was the most companionable of guests, and King Fergus was never tired of his company.

Once when they visited a guard-house the pair over-heard the guard grumbling about a pair of shoes that were given him. He grumbled about their thinness, and Iubdaun laughed to hear him. "Why do you laugh?" Fer-gus said to his little companion. "This man is grumbling about the soles of the shoes given him, and he does not know that, thin as they are, they will outlast his life." And sure enough, the guard quarreled with his comrades and was killed, and in a week another was wearing the shoes which he thought would not give him long enough wear.

It was after this that the seven battalions of the Luprachaun (for we shall call them by this name now, the name by which they are known to us) under the command of Beg, the son of Beg, having crossed the sea, formed themselves upon the lawn of Emain Macha. When King Fergus appeared, their captains shouted:

"We must have Iubdaun—we want our King back with us!"

"I shall not let him return," said the Ulster King.

"Then we shall do a mischief to your people tonight."

"What mischief can you do?"

"We shall loose all the calves in Ulster so that they will go to the cows' udders and leave no milk for the children in the morning."

"That ye may do, but I shall not let Iubdaun go back to you."

The Luprachauns went through the land and untied the halters which held the calves, and the calves went and sucked the cows' milk, and there was none for the children next morning. Again the Luprachauns appeared before Fergus's house, demanding the release of their King, and again the stubborn King of Ulster refused what they pleaded for.

"Then we shall kill all the fish in the streams and rivers," they said.

"That ye may do, but I shall not give Iubdaun back to you."

They went into the streams; they killed salmon, trout and perch, pike, bream, and eel, and even the little minnows in their shoals. In the morning the people found dead fish floating on the tops of the streams and rivers. Again the Luprachauns formed their battalions before the King's house, demanding the return of Iubdaun, and again Fergus stubbornly refused to grant their plea.

"Then we shall cut off the heads of every stalk of grain in Ulster."

"That ye may do, but I shall not let Iubdaun go back to you."

The Luprachauns went into the fields and they cut off the heads of the stalks of wheat, rye, and barley. In the morning, instead of heads of ripening grain the farmers found only stalks standing in their fields. Once more they formed their battalions before King Fergus's house, demanding the release of their King. And once more their plea was refused.

"Then we shall shear the tresses and locks of hair of every man and woman in Ulster," declared Beg, the son of Beg, uttering the Luprachauns' last and most dire threat. "By my word," said Fergus, "if you do any such thing I shall have Iubdaun slain, much as I like him."

He put Iubdaun standing upon his palm so that the battalions of the Luprachaun might have sight of him. Iubdaun commanded Beg, the son of Beg, to halt hostilities. And then he said to Fergus:

> *My spear that a hundred*
> *Men will slay*
> *When the battle tarns*
> *A desperate way—*
>   *Take it, Fergus.*
>
> *My shield that makes safe*
> *The limbs and breast*
> *From stroke or thrust*
> *Where battle's pressed—*
>   *Take it, Fergus.*
>
> *And my silver girdle*
> *That saves from wound,*
> *Or peril, or sickness,*
> *The man it's around—*
>   *Take it, Fergus.*
>
> *And a treasure greater—*
> *The envied wand*

That gives me the love
Of the fair of the land—
      Take it, Fergus.

And my far-brought shoes
That let me tread
The top of the water,
Its depth or its bed—
      Take them, Fergus.

When he heard this count of treasures the King of
Ulster agreed to let Iubdaun ransom himself with one of
them. But he could not make his mind up as to which one
of the treasures he would take as the ransom-price. Then
Iubdaun charged Beg to put the treasures together and to
send them to him by Ae, King Fergus's dwarf. Thereupon
the Luprachauns withdrew to the sea-shore. At the next
break of day they left Ireland, leaving the people lament-
ing the loss of their grain and fish. And once again Fergus
and Iubdaun went about as companions.

In the land of the Luchra and the Luchrapaun, Beg
and Bebo assembled the treasures that Ae was to take
with him to the court of King Fergus. And at the turn
that things had taken the man of lore and learning, Eisirt,
beamed with delight: the wand would be the treasure that
would be taken as ransom for Iubdaun; the wand that

gave the King the love of the ladies of the land would be lost to him. And so in great good-humor Eisirt watched Fergus's dwarf receive the treasures from the Queen and depart with them across the sea.

But each of the treasures was coveted by Fergus: one day he would want the spear, and another day the shield; one day the girdle would seem the treasure worth taking as ransom for Iubdaun, and another day, the wand, and the day after, the shoes made of dragon-skin. So from day to day Iubdaun was kept in his house while the King of Ulster changed from the desire for one possession to the desire for another.

In the end it was the shoes of dragon-skin that Fergus took as the price of Iubdaun's ransom. For a water-monster had appeared in Loch Rudraige, and had given King Fergus so great a fright that his face had become twisted. The King of Ulster saw his face, and saw how twisted it was with the fear he had been put into, and he resolved to go forth and slay the monster that had put this mark of terror on him. On that day King Fergus knew what treasure he desired. He took the shoes that let him tread on the top of the water, or in its depths, or upon its bed, and Iubdaun went out of Ireland, a ransomed King.

He rode on his fairy steed back to the land of the Luchra and the Luchrapaun, his four remaining treasures upon his horse and upon his person, and he found his army drawn up on the shore. The seven battalions raised seven shouts when their King dismounted from his steed; Bebo, his queen, and Beg, his commander, and Glomar, his champion, and Eisirt, his man of lore and learning, and the princes of the Luchra and the Luchrapaun went up to embrace him. A banquet was held in celebration of his return. Iubdaun would not have any heady ale drawn from the vats in the royal cellars; he would not have ale served to his guests and himself, lest with drinking there should come boasting, and with boasting there should come downfall. And so it was at the royal banquets for a year and a day afterwards. In after days, however, when heady ale was drawn from the royal vats and served to the guests at the banquet, a tale would be told of how Beg's seven valiant battalions crossed over to Ireland and forced the King of Ulster to release Iubdaun, the King whom he had unlawfully seized. And that is all that is to be told about the King of the Luchra and the Luchrapaun. And as for the King of Ulster, his name is on a pillar-stone that stands beside Loch Rudraige to this day. The Ogham writing on it tells how King Fergus strove with a water-beast whose fangs wounded him, so that, having slain the beast, he died as he came out of the water. And when they look upon the pillar-stone the people say that treasures forced from the Little People do not bring men the best of fortune.

THE SCHOLAR'S TALE

* * *

THE Scholar put the collar of gold around my neck, and he put the amber that was now polished and strung together in a necklace around the neck of Kevin's daughter, and to the two of us who were under the Big Tree, but feeling that we belonged to some royal palace in the far-back days, he told this story:

KING CORMAC'S CUP

KING Cormac had faults. They were not what would be faults in you or me, but they were faults in a King. In the first place, he believed every tale that was told him. In the second place, he would give anything he had for anything that was brought him. And in the third place, he governed his men of lore and learning very slackly so that they neither did things nor explained things. The first of his faults led to the spread of lying amongst his people.

The second led to the people seeking after new things instead of getting to like the things they had already. And the third fault led to the spread of light-mindedness and want of sense amongst the people. So now you know King Cormac's faults.

But he was a good King, and in those days people knew whether they had or hadn't a good King over them. If they had, wheat grew heavily in the ear, acorns fell thickly in the forest, nuts grew plentifully in the dells, milk poured into the pails, and bees filled their hives with honey. And if they hadn't, they were stinted of wheat, acorns, nuts, milk, and honey. In Cormac's day people had full benefit of field and forest, of dell, dairy, and hive. And he was as fine a figure of a King as you would see in a year and a day's traveling. He stood six feet tall; he had clear gray eyes and a golden beard worn in the fashion that the Kings of Ireland wore their beards.

Well, there stood Cormac, son of Art, looking over the ramparts of Tara on a day of May. So clear and quiet was that first of May that although he was listening to a person who was telling him about the Blue Men of Africa he could have heard the bees humming in the clover-bloom only for the way that his men of lore and learning were disputing with each other and complaining of the ways others had treated them.

Cormac should have worn a royal mantle of crimson

THE SCHOLAR

fringed with gold, but he had given it to someone in exchange for the mantle he had on now—one of green fringed with silver. On his body was a tunic embroidered with gold, and on his feet were sandals of bronze laced with golden thongs, and on his head was his golden crown. Under that crown were the twists and pleats and tassels of his golden beard, and so anyone would know that he was not only a King of Ireland, but the High King of Ireland, and had a right to be standing there and looking over the ramparts of Tara on that May-day.

He saw one coming across the plain who wore the garb and carried the bag of a juggler. And when this one

came to the rampart he saluted the King and the men of
lore and learning, and then, by the King's favor, opened
his bag. He took out, not the balls they expected him
to toss up and catch, but a silver branch on which were
golden apples. He held it up; it was lovely to look at. He
shook it. The golden apples made a peal, and in that peal
there was such music that it seemed to Cormac that all
he ever longed for was beside him. The men of lore and
learning ceased asking riddles and answering them and
they listened, every man of them entranced.

The King cried out, "No!" when the juggler was
about to put the silver branch back into his bag. "The
Bell-branch must remain with me," he said. "Anything
you ask as guerdon for leaving it will be given you—it
will be all that a King can give." "I shall ask three things
in exchange," said the juggler, "and I shall ask for the first
of them when you see me again." He took up the bag;
none were able to tell what direction he took when he left
the ramparts of Tara; he was gone when they came out of
their entrancement.

The King had the Bell-branch. When he shook it
everyone who heard the peal that was made, no matter
what misery they were in before, felt happy with a happiness that they never thought they could have. And if
anyone in Tara was wounded or troubled with disease,
the King had only to shake the Bell-branch and he or she

would fall into an untroubled sleep, and would be sound and well again upon wakening. And so it was in King Cormac's court from May-day to May-day.

And on a May-day he was standing on the ramparts and looking over the plain that stretches from Tara when he saw the juggler coming towards him. He carried no bag, but he wore a very full cloak. The King stepped down to meet him and said, "A guerdon is due to you on account of the Bell-branch you left with me, and this day it shall be given you." Then said the juggler, "Three boons are due to me, and I shall ask for one of them today—Ailbe, your fair young daughter." King Cormac sighed a heavy sigh when he heard this. "A promise is a promise," he said, and he sent for Ailbe. And when she came upon the ramparts he put her hand in the juggler's hand. He, with a sweep of his arm, put his cloak about her, and in a minute the girl and the stranger were gone from the rampart; none of the King's guards knew in what direction they had gone.

When the heavy-hearted King told his wife what had befallen she raised a wail, and when the women knew what the wail was for, they began too, and there was wailing all over Tara. Cormac shook the Bell-branch and the wailing ceased; everyone, even Ailbe's mother, hearing the music of the peal, felt that loss was far from them and happiness beside them. When the music ceased, such was their entrancement, the loss of Ailbe was hardly remembered.

May-day came again, and King Cormac, looking over the ramparts, saw the juggler coming across the plain of Tara, and knew that the second of the boons would be claimed by him. He said, "What would you have from me now?" The juggler answered, "Your son, Cairbre." "A promise is a promise," said King Cormac, "and even this one must be kept." He sent for his son, and when the brave youth stepped to the rampart, Cormac put his hand into the other's hand. Then the juggler flung his cloak about the King's son, and in a minute the pair were gone, and the guards did not know in what direction.

Cormac was heavy-hearted; he told his wife what had befallen and she raised a wail, and when they knew what she was wailing for the women of Tara wailed too, and there was wailing in hall and chamber. But when the Bell-branch was shaken they all became untroubled; all happiness seemed to be beside them, and the loss of Cairbre, like the loss of Ailbe, became a far-away memory. And Cormac himself lost his sadness in his entrancement.

Now although his fair young daughter and his brave young son were reft away from him, King Cormac's life in Tara was as it had been before. Men came to him and told him outlandish stories and he believed them; people showed him things and he gave away what he had so that he might gain them; new men of lore and learning came to his court, and he, instead of setting them to do things or explain things, let them join the others who did nothing but ask riddles and answer riddles and dispute and complain. And when anyone too sorrowfully remembered the loss of Ailbe and Cairbre, or when he remembered their loss himself, the King shook the silver branch and mournfulness left them and left him and happiness was beside them again. And this was the way in Tara until another May-day came round.

The King saw the juggler coming towards where he stood looking over the ramparts, and mournfulness came upon him, for he remembered that the third of the boons promised had still to be given him. And when the juggler came and stood beside him at the rampart, Cormac said, "Ask for your boon and it shall be given you, for a promise is a promise." "A promise is a promise," the juggler said, "and I have come to get the third boon promised me. I ask you to let me have Eithne, your wife."

The King, setting command upon himself, sent for his wife; when she came he put her hand in the other's hand. Then the juggler flung his cloak about her, and in a minute he and she were gone, and Cormac who had been alone by the ramparts did not know what direction they had gone in. He groaned heavily. But he knew that groaning was no use, and taking his sword in his hand and filled with a great passion of grief and anger, he sprang off the ramparts of Tara and ran across the plain.

The clear light of May-day had been on everything, but as he went on a mist fell down or rose up. It was light at first and was only about his feet, but it became heavier and thicker and thicker and heavier. He heard birds' cries coming through it. He went on and on and came suddenly out of the mist. And now a lovely light was upon everything. But the plain he was on was strange to Cormac. The grass was bright; there were white blossoms on the hawthorns and golden blossoms on the furze, and there was the singing of larks above, but on that wide plain there was neither hill nor bush nor rock nor tree that he remembered.

And then he saw where dwellings were. He went towards them and saw that surrounding them was a rampart of bronze with an opening through it. Within the rampart the dwellings stood as palaces, one having every embellishment, and the other without thatch as yet upon it. There was a well of springing water before the opening of the rampart—water so bright and clear that Cormac stood looking into it for a long space of time.

Around that well nine hazel trees grew; their leaves looked as if they never withered, and their branches bore purple nuts that fell into the water. As one fell, a silver salmon, one of the five that were in the well, rose and fed on it and then swam down one of the five streams that flowed out of the well. A salmon with a shining body having fed on a purple nut went swimming down each of the streams that in their flowing made a murmur that was as sweet as music. As King Cormac listened to that murmur and looked into the clearness of the water he felt close to an understanding of something that he had not understood heretofore—something was rising in his mind like the bubbles that came to the top of the well as the salmon rose and fed on the nuts that fell to them from the branches of the hazel trees.

He went within the rampart and he looked on the palace that as yet was without thatch upon its roof. He was not the only one who was before it; riders kept coming to it bearing bags; in the bags were feathers of birds of all kinds. They handed the bags of feathers to men who, on the top of the palace, were engaged in thatching the roof. These men put down the black and white and speckled feathers to make a thatch. But they stayed their work to dispute with each other, and gusts of wind came and blew the feathers from under their hands, so that no matter how many bags were handed to them the thatch was never laid to more than a few hands' breadth. All around where King Cormac stood feathers were flying; on the ground was a depth of feathers which gusts of wind took up and blew away. Looking on the feathers and on the men who were letting them flow from them, King Cormac felt as if he were reaching to an understanding of something—he did not know what.

He turned to the palace that was embellished, and the doorkeepers who were there led him within. In the hall was a couch on which a noble-looking man was seated. He rose as Cormac entered and brought him to the couch and sat beside him. A basin of water was at his feet and a servant was ready to bathe them. But where the basin had come from, or how the heating-stones had been placed in or taken out of the water, Cormac did not know. The noble-looking personage who was the lord of the palace conversed with him, and all he said brought Cormac closer and closer to the understanding that was forming in his mind.

His feet bathed, he felt refreshed. A broad-shouldered man, the meat of a pig across his shoulders and an ax and a log of wood in his hands, came into the hall. "It is time to prepare a meal," said the lord, "for a noble guest is with us." Then the man split the log and lighted a fire on the hearth and hung the pig to cook before the fire. And Cormac marveled as he looked upon the hearth because, although great heat came from the fire, the wood did not seem to burn away.

Said the lord of the palace, "It is time to turn what cooks before the fire." "Not so," said the broad-shouldered man, "for if the pig were roasting forever it would not be cooked until, for every quarter of it, a true tale is told." "Do you, then," said the lord to Cormac, "tell us a true tale."

Then King Cormac told how his daughter, his son, and his wife had been lost to him, and how, rushing out to take back his wife, he had lost himself and had wandered through a mist, and how he had come to the place they were in. And when he had finished this tale the broad-shouldered man turned what was roasting before the fire, and behold! a quarter of the pig was cooked perfectly. "A true tale you have told," said the lord of the palace. And then he said:

"The season for plowing had come, but when we went to the field we found it plowed and harrowed and sown with seed. The harvest came on; we went to reap but found the grain already stacked in sheaves. When we went to bring the sheaves home we found the field cleared and the sheaves made into a rick and the rick thatched. Since that time we have been thrashing and grinding sheaves out of that rick, and yet the rick is never any less." And when the lord of the palace had told this the broad-shouldered man turned what was roasting, and, behold! another quarter of the pig was cooked. "A true story you have told," said the man.

A lady had come in and had seated herself beside the

lord of the palace. She was asked to tell a true tale, and she said, "I own seven cows and seven sheep, and from my cows I draw enough milk to feed all the people of this land, and from my sheep I shear enough wool to clothe all of them." When she told this the man turned the pig and another quarter of it was cooked. "A true tale you have told," said the lord of the palace to the lady, and then he said to the broad-shouldered man, "Tell how you came into possession of the log and the ax."

"One day," said the broad-shouldered man, "I found a strange cow grazing in a field of mine. I took her and tied her in the cattle-pound. Her owner came searching for her, and he offered me a reward for letting him take her out of the pound. I let him take the cow and he gave me this ax and this log of wood. No matter how long it burns the wood is never consumed, and when I strike the logs with the back of the ax they become a whole log again." Then he turned what was roasting before the fire, and, behold! the pig was cooked through and through. "A true tale you have told," said the lord of the palace. And then to Cormac he said, "You know now what land you are in." "It is the Land of Wonders."

"It is Tir Tairngire, the Land of Promise," said the lord of the palace.

The pig being cooked the meat was laid on a dish and carried to the table. "You will eat now," said the lord of the palace to Cormac. "By your favor," said Cormac, "but I never sit down to meat unless there is a company of fifty to share it with me." Then the lord of the palace called aloud, and straightaway a company came into the hall and seated themselves at the table. And when Cormac sat down, lo! there was his son one side of him and his daughter the other side, and his wife was seated across from him. Great joy came over him, but before he could speak or make a sign the lord of the palace had filled a golden cup and had passed it to him. And when King Cormac drank what was in the cup all the anxiety he had had went from him, and he only knew that his wife and daughter and son were with him, and that all was well with them and with him.

They drank from the golden cup, all who were at the table, and Cormac, looking closely at the lord of the palace, saw that he was the same person as the juggler who had given him the silver branch and had taken away his daughter, his son, and his wife. "Tell me the meaning of this," he said. Thereupon the lord of the palace told him:

"The well you looked into is the Well of Wisdom and its five streams are the five senses that men have. All who would practice science or art must drink out of that well or out of the streams that flow from it. And from now on you will be able to recognize those who have drunk out of the well or the streams. And when you have recognized them and shown them that you have recognized them they will not spend their time disputing and complaining. Those whom you saw thatching the roof and never finishing their task are the men of lore and learning who spend their days in useless disputations. These, too, you will be able to recognize; I brought you here so that you might behold and understand these things.

"And I who speak to you am the Lord of Ocean and the Warden of Ireland, Manannan MacLir." As he spoke he held in his hands the golden cup, and Cormac marveled at the workmanship that was shown on it. "But its marvel is," said Manannan, "that if a falsehood is uttered over it the cup breaks into pieces, and if a truth is told over it it becomes whole again." And then he told a story about Cormac that was not true, and the cup broke into three pieces. "Your wife and daughter, since they left Tara," said he after the breaking of the cup, "never looked on the face of a man until they came into this hall, and your son never looked on a woman's face." When he said this the cup became whole again. Manannan placed it in Cormac's hand. "You will give me the silver branch with the golden apples on it for this," he said to him.

In Manannan's chariot they drove through the mist— Cormac, his wife with their son and daughter. They came before the rampart of Tara, and when they went within great were the rejoicings over each and every one of them.

The silver branch with the golden apples went back to the Land of Promise. The golden cup was placed on the King's board. And thereafter those who thought they could tell any story and be believed by Cormac were often surprised to see the cup break into three pieces when their words were said, and were then dismayed when they were told that they would have to tell a true story about themselves to make the cup whole again. Truth-telling caught up on lying and passed it. Also choice was made amongst the men of lore and learning who presented themselves, and those who were chosen did things and explained things in such a way that the people began to understand what art was and science was, and understanding this they became less light-minded and more sensible. And Cormac no more gave away the things he had for the things that were brought him, and this made everybody grow to like the things they had. The golden cup was always upon his board. But when King Cormac died it disappeared, and its like has not been seen in Ireland since his day.

WHILE WE ATE GOOSEBERRIES

* * *

ONE day I found the Scholar again under the Big Tree. He called out to me: "Buy me a penny-worth of gooseberries of the Apple-woman's cart and buy a penny-worth for yourself at the same time. And here you're back, and what a lot of gooseberries, to be sure, can still be got for twopence! Sit beside me here, and if you want a story I'll tell you one while we're eating our gooseberries. Indeed, I'll tell you two, for I'll tell you the story that shattered King Cormac's cup, and the story that put it together again.

THE STORY THAT SHATTERED KING CORMAC'S CUP AND THE STORY THAT PUT IT TOGETHER AGAIN

HE wasn't an Eirinach, but a Britainach—a man of Britain—who told King Cormac the first story. The man said, said he:

"As I went looking for the Mill that's called the Grind-'Em-Young, I came to a Blacksmith's Forge, and over it was written THE WONDER SMITH AND HIS SON. I wondered what wonders were wrought there, and I went in to see. The young Smith was working the bellows as I came in. He blew the fire into a blaze, and then he blew out of the blaze—what would you have?—a shower of wheat that lay deep upon the floor of the forge. Then the old Smith went to the bellows. He blew and he blew and he blew out of the blaze—what would you have?—a flock of pigeons. They settled down on the floor and ate up every grain of the wheat that was there, and then they all disappeared.

"Then the young Smith went to the bellows and he blew and he blew, and he blew out of the blaze—what would you have?—a fine salmon. It leaped into the little stream that was flowing by the door of the forge, and swam out of sight.

"Then said the old Smith, 'I must have that salmon brought back again or the man who has come in will not believe that I can work wonders.' So he went to the bellows and with might and main he worked it. Out of the blaze he blew—what would you have?—an active-looking

THE YOUNG SMITH WENT TO THE BELLOWS AND HE BLEW
OUT OF THE BLAZE——A FINE SALMON.

otter. He sprang into the stream, and swimming down it
came back with the salmon in his mouth. He laid it down
on the floor of the forge. I went to look at it, but as I did
it leaped into the fire. And when I turned round again the
otter had disappeared.

"And now I had seen wonders enough, and I went
out of the Forge and along by the stream until I came
to where the river flowed, and there I saw a Mill, and
over it was written I GRIND 'EM YOUNG AGAIN. This was
the Grind-'Em-Young, and I knew that if I went into it

I would be ground and ground until old age was ground out of my bones and that then I should be young again. But the crowd of young men coming out of it was such that I was crushed against the wall of the bridge..."

(It was then that King Cormac's Cup broke in three pieces. And in three pieces it remained until the son of the King of Connacht, Prince Conneda, told King Cormac this story.)

Prince Conneda said, said he:

"My mother died soon after I was born, and on her death-bed she asked the King, my father, to have me brought up in a tower that was a distance from his royal castle, and to have no one tell anything of me, good or bad, until I had reached manhood's years. My mother did this because she feared that my father would wed again, and that his new Queen, out of jealousy of me, would find some way of ending my life. Well, to the tower I was sent, and in that tower which was far from the royal castle I was reared, and those who waited on me were all speechless people. My father had this done, although he took no new Queen for years after my mother's death.

"He married again. I was near to my manhood's years when the new Queen was brought to my father's castle. No word reached her about my being in the world. A son was born to her and she thought that he was heir to my father's kingdom.

"Now one day the Queen was walking by the border of the forest and she met the Herb-woman with the basket of herbs she had gathered. 'May you never come this way again,' said the Herb-woman to her. The Queen was amazed to hear her speak as if she was cursing her, and said, 'Down on your knees and beg my forgiveness or I shall have your head taken off!' The Herb-woman went down on her knees before the Queen. 'It was a prayer, not a curse I spoke,' she said, 'and if you'll have the reason for my making such a prayer you'll have to pay high for it.' 'How much will I have to pay?' asked the Queen. 'As much wool as will fill my wool-sack, as much butter as will fill my crock, as much wheat as will fill my chest.' 'And how much will all these be, Herb-woman?' asked the Queen. 'To fill my wool-sack will take seven sheep and their increase for seven years, to fill my crock will take seven cows and their increase for seven years, to fill my chest will take seven barrels of wheat and their increase for seven years.' 'It is a great price.' 'A great price indeed it is, and I should not ask for it if what I have to tell you did not concern you so much.' 'Tell me, and the price you ask will be given you.' 'I prayed that you might never come this way again,' said the Herb-woman, 'because if you do you will one day come to the tower where Prince Conneda, the heir to the kingdom, resides.' 'Is my son, then, not his father's heir, and the heir to the kingdom?' cried the Queen. 'No. The King had another Queen before your time; the Prince is now near to the years of manhood, and he it is who is heir to the kingdom; yonder is the gray tower that he lives in.' 'You must tell me, Herb-woman, what I must do to gain the kingdom for my son?' 'Have your steward bring me the seven sheep, the seven cows, and the seven barrels of wheat, with the pledge that their increase shall be mine for seven years, and I shall show you what you must do.' And when this was told to her the Queen turned back to the castle, letting the Herb-woman go on her own path.

"That very evening the steward brought to the Herb-woman's hut the seven cows, the seven sheep, and the seven barrels of wheat, with the Queen's pledge that she should have their increase for seven years. The Queen met her on the forest path next morning. 'Tell me now what I must do to keep my son heir to his father's kingdom?' 'Prince Conneda will reach manhood's years on the May-day coming. Have his father invite him to supper with you in the royal castle, and then entice him to play a game of cards with you. Here is the pack to play with—an enchanted pack of cards. And when you have won the game as you will assuredly win it, lay your command upon him that he is not to sleep a night in the tower or the castle until he brings to you the Wild Steed of Bells from the stable of the Dismal Knight of the Glens.'

"That night the young Queen told the old King laughingly that she had known ever since she wedded him that he had a son besides the one that was in the cradle. She asked him to invite the Prince to supper with her on the night of the day that he reached manhood's years. The old King rejoiced to find her so good-humored about the secret she had discovered; besides, he wanted to see me in his castle on the day I reached manhood's years. So he agreed to invite me to supper on the night of May-day.

"I came. I sat beside the Queen. Her beauty and her kindness led me to think that everything she said and did was just and right. And so when she asked me to play a game of cards with her I did so with all the good-will in the world. I lost the game. I asked her what forfeit I should pay. 'The King must hear it,' she said, and she wakened my father out of his doze. 'It is,' she said in his full hearing, 'that you, Prince Conneda, go forth this night and return not to tower or castle without bringing me the Wild Steed of Bells out of the stable of the Dismal Knight of the Glens.'

"My father fell back on his cushions when he heard this, and when I saw the smile that was on the lips of the Queen and the gleam that was in her eyes I knew what dangers were before me. But there was nothing for me to do except comfort my father and take his blessing and depart from his castle. So I turned from the Queen and went forth to venture my life on getting the Wild Steed of Bells out of the stable of the Dismal Knight of the Glens.

"As I went on my way the next day I met a supple-looking old man who wore a black cap; he saluted me as I saluted him, and when I asked him to show me the way to the Glens he answered that he would come with me. 'You may call me the Champion with the Black Cap, Prince Conneda,' he said, 'and I hope I shall prove of use to your father's son.'

"We went together, the Champion with the Black Cap and myself, and we went into the depths of the dark Glen where the Dismal Knight had his habitation. As we pushed open the first gate we fell into a pit that was prepared for all who might venture near the stable, and there we lay until the sergeants of the Knight of the Glens took us before their master.

"And when it was shown to the Dismal Knight of the Glens that we had come to steal his Wild Steed of Bells he bade his sergeants fasten to the beam of the roof the rope that was to hang us; I was to be the first to have the rope put round my neck. The noose was lowered to where I stood and the Dismal Knight said to me, 'There are only three minutes between yourself and death.' 'There were only two minutes between myself and death at one time,' said the Champion with the Black Cap, 'and I am here to tell you about it.' 'If what you say is true,' said the Knight of the Glens, 'you must have been in as great a danger as man ever was before.' 'I was, and I have lived to tell about it, and so shall this Prince. If I prove that this was so will you spare the life of this young man?' 'I will, although it is my custom to hang from the beam of my hall anyone who comes to try to steal my Wild Steed of Bells.'

"Then said the Champion with the Black Cap:

"'Once when I was upon my travels I got lost upon a moor and I went towards where I saw smoke rising. The minute I came before it I knew it belonged to witches because I could smell the ointment they rub upon themselves. But, bravely enough, I went inside, thinking I could get a cup of water and go on my way before they got into any fury with me. A woman was there with a child on her lap, and I knew that she was not harmful. "What has brought you into the Witches' House?" said she. "What has brought you into the same house?" said I. "I have been carried here with the child whose nurse I am and the Witches will do some evil to him. The three of them are away at the moment, but soon they will be back, and I dread what will be done then to the child." "Why do you not run off with him?" "It would do no good to run off. They have fastened a ring on the child's finger, and as I go across the moor with him they will call out "Ring, where are you?' and the ring will answer, "Here I am." And so they can track me down, and then they will kill me for trying to make an escape. And the three are coming now," she said, "and if you wish to be safe you will make away."

"'I snatched the child from her lap and I ran out of the door. The Witches were coming but the dusk was falling and I thought I could get to where I could hide in the darkness and so save myself and the child. I went towards where trees were growing together. I climbed up one of them with the child holding to me, his arms round my neck. And when I got amongst the branches of the trees I thought that the Witches would not be able to find me or that they would not be able to climb to where the child and I were.

"'But as they crossed the moor they called out, "Ring, where are you?" and the ring on the child's finger answered, "Here I am." Then they came to the tree and looked up to where we were with their cat-like eyes. But could they climb the tree? They could not, and they could not stay there until daylight, either. Still, Witches the like of these Witches are not to be baffled by man's devices. One of them changed herself into an ax-head, the other changed herself into an ax-handle, while the third fitted the handle into the head and began to swing the ax against the tree. The tree shook with the blows she struck against it, and more and more did her ax cut into the trunk. And while she cut into the tree she called out, "Ring, where are you?" and the ring would answer, "Here am I."

"'I knew what to do to save myself and the child. I cut off the finger that the ring was on and flung it into the lake that was some distance from the trees. "Ring, where are you?" called the Witch. "Here am I," said the ring, speaking out of the water of the lake. She did not wait to think how we could have got into the water, but with the ax in her hands, she rushed over and plunged into the lake. She was drowned and so were her two sisters who were in the forms of the ax-handle and the ax-head.

"'I had to be very spry getting down that tree with the child's arms around my neck; the trunk was nearly cut through, and if I had leaned heavily on one side or the other it would have crashed down, killing myself or the child, or, maybe, both of us. However, I got my feet upon firm ground, and I went back to the Witches' house and found the child's nurse there. I gave him back to her; she put some of the Witches' ointment where the finger had been cut off and healed the wound that was made. I went on my way then, and my travels and adventures would keep me talking to you from this until breakfast-time. But you will see that I was closer to my death than the young Prince is who has the rope's noose resting on his shoulder.'

"Said the Dismal Knight of the Glens, 'I acknowledge that you were, and the young man's life is spared him, but you and he will have to go from where I keep my Wild Steed of Bells.' And no sooner had he said this than the old woman who was seated on a heap of rushes by the hearth spoke up and said: 'The deeds of the Champion with the Black Cap were as true as his words are. I was the nurse in whose charge the the child who was carried off by the three Witches. And,' said she, turning to the Dismal Knight of the Glens, 'you were that child. I reared you until you came into possession of your father's lands and titles, and the reason you are called the Dismal Knight is because you always have a memory of the ax-blows upon the tree.' 'Indeed you are right,' said Knight of the Glens, 'for not only have I lacked a finger since childhood, but every night I think of the shaking tree. I'll not think of it again,' he said, 'and I'll be known no more as the Dismal Knight.' And then he said to me, 'Not only will I let you go free but I shall bestow upon you my Wild Steed of Bells.' He called to the grooms and he had them lead the Steed out of the stable, and holding him by the horse-block he bade me mount him and ride back to my father's castle. 'But call to see me now and again,' he said to me, 'so that we may get to know each other better.'

"I rode from the Glens upon the Steed of Bells and the Champion with the Black Cap ran beside me. It was good going with thud of hooves and peal of bells that brought me through the green wood where my lonesome tower stood. But my step-mother was on its top. When she heard the bells and knew I had the steed with me she fell from its height and lost her life that minute. I went to my father's castle bringing the Champion with me, and I was declared heir to the Kingdom of Connacht. And here I am, King Cormac, to ask for your good-will when I take the Kingship."

(And when Prince Conneda had told this story, the Cup that was shattered in three pieces was made whole again.)

PATCH THE NAILER

* * *

I was going away. I would not be coming into Bunlahy again. Not on errands, anyway. Not for tea nor sugar nor salt; not for baking soda nor currants for a cake; not for snuff nor candles. I sat under the Big Tree and wondered at myself for being so extraordinary as to be leaving a place where the only people I knew would keep on living. Where there would be a Bone-fire that I would not be there to see. And where the young crows and jackdaws would be falling out of their nests in spring, and hopping in the grass inside and outside of Baron's Court, and I would not be there to catch one of them and keep it as a pet bird as I always had intended to do. I would be a boy without any pet crow or pet jackdaw, or, for that matter, without any mother or grandmother to live with or to do errands for. It was certain I was extraordinary. But there was no one in Bunlahy to come up to me and acknowledge that. There might have been had it been any other day, but this day there was a meeting somewhere with speeches and bands and there was hardly a soul in the village but had gone off to it. It is true that when I had brought back the smoothing-iron that my mother had borrowed again from her, the woman in the shop that sold pins and needles (Mrs. Dunphy was her name) had given me a penny lucky-bag, but that, I thought, was because I had said a prayer that she might be led to do that, and not because anything was due to the fact that I had become an extraordinary person. I said everybody was gone out of Bunlahy that day. But everybody did not include Patch the Nailer who never left the village and very seldom stepped outside his little forge. I could hear his hammer ringing on his little anvil as he beat out a long nail—a holdfast it was called. I had looked in at him as I went by on my way to Mrs. Dunphy's, and had noticed his little forge-fire that was about as big as a candle-flame, and the little anvil, and the pieces of metal on the ground, and the bench covered with nails and spikes, and the irons hanging on the cobwebbed walls that might, for all anybody knew about them, be some rare inventions of Patch's own, and Patch himself hammering as he was always hammering, and the stair that went up to the room that he slept in and that must have been as queer a place as the forge was only that nobody had ever seen it. The ringing sound stopped and Patch now pushed open the door and came out on the street. He looked a bit blinky as he well might, for the full daylight wasn't his element. He saw me and came over to where I was under the tree. "Patch," I told him, "I won't be coming into Bunlahy again." One of his eyes was dimmed but the other one was bright and roving, and he looked at me reckoningly with his eyes. He had on a leather apron, and the soot was in the wrinkles of his face (when I used to see him at Mass with his face washed I thought he was a different man from Patch the Nailer). He gave me an apple (but where Patch could have got an apple I couldn't guess), and he said, "I think that, like the Spaeman, you'll come back to the Big Tree." "Tell me what he did," said I, and Patch the Nailer sat under the Big Tree (the first time he was outside his forge in many a long day) and told me:

THE STORY OF THE SPAEMAN

ONCE upon a time and a very good time it was, though I had neither hat nor shoe, nor coat nor cloak, with a stick in my hand and a stone under my foot I went on my way to the Parish of No-sense where everyone has a goose for a gossip. Up hill and down dale and through the boggy, miry places I went, for it was only in the Parish of No-sense that I could better the state I was in. But when I came to Goose-green that is in the middle of the parish the doors were closed and the rushlights were dowsed, and there was no one in sight that I could crave shelter of. I walked between the mill and the moat and the moat and the mill, harkening for the watchman's "All's well! All's well," but they had neither watchman nor warden in the Parish of No-sense. I went through a broken door and into an empty house and I lay down to sleep upon the cold hearthstones. And while I was lying there in the deep darkness three knaves came in. They were carrying bags and bundles of stuffs they had stolen and they had come to hide them in the empty bins that were left in the house. And they went tiptoeing and whispering and telling each other that they would bring the brown mare and the gray horse and the spavined jennet and load the stuffs upon them and get out of the town next day when the dusk was falling.

When daylight came I got up from where I lay and went and warmed myself at a hearth I was asked to and ate out of the porridge-pot, and then I made my way to Goose-green which is the center of the parish to hear of what doings might be in the town. And no sooner had I got there when the Bellman came up and ringing his bell gave out that goods had been stolen and that a reward would be given to whoever discovered the thieves. All on Goose-green talked about this happening: some said that and some said this, "What we want in this town is a Spaeman who could know by his own insight where stolen things are taken to. If we had a Spaeman we'd have no robberies here, and the town should hire one." And they all said, "Hear, hear!" to this, and so I went where the Bellman was drinking his dram, and I took up the bell that he had laid down on the ground, and I went through Goose-green crying, "A Spaeman am I, a Spaeman am I, and what town wants to hire a man with insight enough to know where stolen things are hidden!" They said I would have to prove I was a Spaeman before they hired me, and they took me to the warehouse that the robbery was made from (Peter's in Duck Street) and they asked me what my insight showed me. "It shows me," I said, "that three robbers took bags and bundles of stuffs from this place, and that the same robbers will be leaving the town at dusk carrying their loads upon a brown mare, a gray horse, and a spavined jennet."

They set a watch upon the bridge, and as dusk fell along came a brown mare, a gray horse, and a spavined jennet with loads of stuffs upon them and a man walking beside each load. The watch with their staves in their hands surrounded the beasts and the men, but the robbers jumped over the bridge and ran away. The stolen goods were found in the packs that the mare, the horse, and the jennet carried, and they were brought back to the warehouse. "The best Spaeman that ever was," the people said about me, and they gave me a house to live in and a penny a day pension and a candle to light my chamber in the night-time and free entry to all the games and cock-fights that might be on Goose-green. So there I lived in comfort and security, not having to make any more discoveries, for when they knew that the town had a Spaeman wrongdoers went to other places.

But I got tired of a place where there were no doings, for although I had free entry to the games and cock-fights upon Goose-green it was no good, for none ever took place there. So when the Squire asked me to come to his place and be Spaeman for him, I left my house with its candle-light and my penny a day pension and went to his mansion. His silver was being taken, spoon by spoon and plate by plate, and there was no way of finding out who was taking it or where it was being taken to. And when I came to the door, there were the butler and the footman and the groom, all with long faces on them, telling the Squire that the potato-ring and the salt-cellar had disappeared. "This day must not pass," said the Squire to me, "without your discovering for me where my silver is being taken to."

I was sorry I came, for the insight I had wasn't likely to tell me where the Squire's silver was being taken to. Howsomever, I thought I should get a meal out of my visit to the mansion. So I told the Squire that I couldn't engage in the matter until I had a meal with no less than three pots of ale to go with it. So a dish of duck was set before me in a room next the pantry. I took up knife and fork and looked for the pot of ale that wasn't there. And just then the butler came out of the pantry with the pot in his hand. "Here comes the first of them," I said aloud, and the butler gave a start and put the pot before me with a shaking hand.

I heard him talking to the footman and the groom in the pantry and it seemed to me that his voice was very failing. Then the footman came in with a pot in his hand. "Here comes the second of them," I said aloud, and he gave such a start that he spilled the ale on me as he set it down and went out of the room before I could give him a second look.

I drank my ale and I ate my duck, and I could hear them talking in the pantry and their voices sounded strained as two were saying to the third, "You go to him now." So the groom came in carrying the ale-pot, and I said aloud, "Here comes the third and the last of them." The groom let the pot fall and the ale went on the floor. He went back into the pantry without a word, and the next thing I saw was the three servants standing before me. The butler spoke to me and said, "You know us and we were foolish to think that you would not discover us as you discovered us before when we stole the bundles of cloth. And now what will you take not to inform on us?"

"All I want," I said, "is to see the place where the silver's hidden, and if that's shown to me you can go from the mansion without my informing on you."

They took me to the cellar then and there and they showed me where they had hidden the silver until such time as they could get it safely away. I waited until they had gone helter-skelter, and then I sat down at the table, picking a bone and drinking a dram from the pot. The Squire came to me. "What have you to tell me, Spaeman?" he asked. "Go down to the cellar, move over the biggest of the hogsheads, and you'll find an opening under it and there's where your silver is, if I amn't mistaken." So he went down with the coachman and moved over the hogshead, and there was his silver, plate and spoon, salt-cellar and potato-ring.

The Squire declared that I was the best Spaeman that ever was, and he gave me a gate-lodge to live in and sixpence a day and leave to come in and talk with the gentlemen after dinner and drink what they offered me. And one night when I was in the dining-room drinking a punch with a gentleman I heard the Squire making a bet with another gentleman that I could find out anything about anything that was put before me. "I lay you five thousand pounds that he will not be able to find out what's in a dish that I'll put before him," said the gentleman. "Done," said the Squire, and then he turned to me and said, "Spaeman, my fortune's wagered on your insight. Win you must, and when you do I'll reward you well." I was very frightened to hear this, and I would have stolen away from the place only the Squire had me stay in the mansion that night so as to be ready for the trial that was to take place next afternoon.

I lay awake all night. I knew the name I had for being a Spaeman wouldn't last out the trial that was before me, and I knew that the Squire was going to lose his fortune, and that I would lose my sixpence a day and my place in the gate-lodge. I didn't leave my bed until all was ready for the trial. The gentleman had prepared a dish of meat and I was to taste it and then tell all present what beast it was cut from. The Squire and his friend and the gentleman who had made the bet were all seated at the table when I came in, my knees knocking together. I had a look of great anxiety from the Squire, and I was afraid to give him a look back. Then, I can tell you, I cursed the day when I had given myself out for a Spaeman.

The cover-dish was taken off and there in the dish was a stew of meat. "Speak up and tell us what it is," said the gentleman who had made the bet. What was it? Beef or mutton, pork or goat, veal or venison, rabbit or hare? I was less able to tell than anyone in the world, for all sense of smell or taste had gone from me with the fright I was in. "You can't tell what it is," said the gentleman, looking at me as if the Squire's five thousand pounds were in his pocket already. "Your honor," I said, "the old fox is caught at last." At that he dropped the cover-dish he was holding. "No one else could have known," he said, "that this is the fox that was caught yesterday, for I cut him up and cooked him with my own hands." And when he said this the Squire came up and took my own two hands and shook them till the blood was nearly squeezed out of them.

More than before I had the name of being a Spaeman. But my last feat did me little good, for, with the money he won, the Squire went traveling, and when he was gone a full year the steward stopped my sixpence a day, and in a while after that he turned me out of the gate-lodge to let a young couple who were relations of his live there. So back I went to the Parish of No-sense and stood upon Goose-green and cried out that I was a Spaeman and that I could be hired. But the young people who were there asked me what a Spaeman was, and when I told them they laughed and said that they could make discoveries by insight themselves. As is the way with people, they had become more foolish than their fathers. So I said, say I—

Let them go to the Devil and shake themselves,
And when they come back, behave themselves.

So without hat or shoe, coat or cloak, and with a stick in my hand and a stone under my foot I went from the Parish of No-sense. Over hills and down dales I went, and through miry, boggy places, and came back to where I had started from—

The Tree That Withstood
The Big
Wind—The
Big Tree of Bunlahy.

CLUNY MEDIA

Designed by Fiona Cecile Clarke, the CLUNY MEDIA *logo
depicts a monk at work in the scriptorium,
with a cat sitting at his feet.*

*The monk represents our mission to emulate
the invaluable contributions of the monks
of Cluny in preserving the libraries of the West,
our strivings to know and love the truth.*

*The cat at the monk's feet is Pangur Bán, from the
eponymous Irish poem of the 9th century.
The anonymous poet compares his scholarly
pursuit of truth with the cat's happy hunting of mice.
The depiction of Pangur Bán is an homage to the work
of the monks of Irish monasteries and a sign
of the joy we at Cluny take in our trade.*

"Messe ocus Pangur Bán,
cechtar nathar fria saindan:
bíth a menmasam fri seilgg,
mu memna céin im saincheirdd."

Made in the USA
Middletown, DE
26 January 2025

70153979R00116